CHAOS AND ASH

FIRE WITCHES OF SALEM
BOOK ONE

CARRIE PULKINEN

ISBN: 978-1-957253-12-1

CHAPTER

ONE

People loved to claim they were descendants of the witches they couldn't burn. We actually were. Our ancestors literally could not be set on fire. Neither could we. My sisters and I were elemental witches, and fire was ours to command. The veil between worlds was thin in Salem, and we belonged to the order of witches duty-bound to keep the monsters at bay.

We were the Veil Keepers.

Yep, the witches were the ones that kept Salem safe. Ironic, right? It had always been that way too. Good thing my ancestors couldn't burn, or this town—and everything around it—would've been screwed six ways to Sunday a long, long time ago.

Of course, they didn't burn witches in Salem.

Everyone knew that. They hanged them here, pressed one of them to death, but my family originated in England. Back in the sixteen hundreds, my great-great-who-knows-how-many-greats-grandma was tied to a stake and set on fire. Well, the wood around her was set ablaze. The flames incinerated her clothes, and when the inferno extinguished, Granny stood there naked and unscathed, laughing at the astonished looks on their faces.

Man, I would've loved to have seen that. She might or might not have set the village on fire to make her escape. The details didn't matter. The important thing was that we were here in our little shop on the edge of downtown, preparing to take out yet another horde of monsters to keep safe the very people who would have murdered us four hundred years ago.

Fun times.

My sister Ember laid her forearm across the table, and I dipped my needle into the enchanted ink. Closing my eyes, I focused my energy, drawing from the goddess and infusing the sigil I was about to create with my vim.

"You're raiding a vampire nest, right? So, speed and strength?" With my fingers wrapped firmly around the grip, I pressed the tip of the needle against her skin and drew the first line.

"Vampire ghouls, but yeah."

Ick. There were two different levels of vamps in the world. First, the so-called normal kind, who could pass as humans. They still fried in the sunlight, but at night, a mundane wouldn't know them from one of their own. The other kind, ghouls, were disgusting. Imagine if a zombie and a vampire had a baby and the zombie traits were the dominant ones. Mindless, bloodsucking monsters. My lip curled at the thought.

"Throw in a bit of protection, and I'll be set." Ember smiled, but her eyes were tight.

I pressed a little harder, clenching my teeth. "You know I don't do those."

She winced. "You could."

"I can't."

"I wish you had more self-confidence. You broke the family curse for Hecate's sake."

That much was true. Another witch cursed our bloodline centuries ago. The third daughter of every Holland mother would die in infancy. Once birth control became a thing, our ancestors stopped after two kids rather than risk losing a little girl. Well, they tried to anyway. My mom's pill failed, and I was the result. Somehow, she managed to keep me alive into adulthood, breaking the curse, but that didn't mean I was some kind of prophet or whatever. I got lucky. Nothing more.

I turned off the machine and sat back in my chair.

"The last thing I need is you going into a vampire nest thinking you've got protection when you don't. I never mastered that sigil, and Cinder paid the price. I can't lose you too."

A shadow crossed her features, her gaze shifting downward before meeting mine. "We're going to find her."

"Are we? She searched for Mom and Dad for months, insisting they were alive, and now she's gone too. Who's next? You or me? We won't find her."

Her jaw tightened. I couldn't tell you how many times we'd had this conversation, yet no matter where we looked or what we tried, our sister had vanished, and I was to blame.

"Okay. Speed and strength will do." She pressed her lips together, giving me what she probably thought was an expression of sympathy.

It looked like pity to me, and I was not having it. I picked up the machine and returned to her sigil, losing myself in the rhythmic pulse of the needles. I'd be lying if I said I didn't take a tiny bit of pleasure in knowing these things hurt like a bitch. It was "no pain, no gain" in the most literal sense.

Black ink penetrated her skin, the faint blue glow indicating my magic was infusing her with the desired properties. Okay, it wasn't all my magic. Mostly, I chan-neled the goddess and the power of the universe, the energy traveling into me and out through the enchanted ink. But my vim went into every sigil I tattooed, and it took a while to recharge when I'd done a lot, like tonight.

Ember was my last canvas out of five in the past hour. With a hunting party that big, they must've been expecting a slew of bloodsuckers to come out of that nest.

The fatigue was worth it to do my part. Goddess knew I couldn't fight a monster to save my life. That was why I was the coven librarian and Ember was the badass butt kicker.

"If you're not covered in vampire goo when you're done, do you want to have a drink at the Twisted Thistle?" I shook the tension from my hand before putting the finishing touch on her sigil, bringing the bottom loop down and around like the tail of a cursive G, ending it with a fine point, exactly how my dad had taught me.

She scrunched her nose. "I made plans with Shade and Chrys. Sorry."

"Oh." I tried to hide the disappointment in my voice, but I failed miserably. "That's okay. I should head to bed early, anyway. I'm re-cataloging the grimoires tomorrow. Dad's organizational skills were lacking at best. He never reshelved anything in the right place."

The back door opened, and Shade poked his head

in. "Hurry it up in there. The sun's about to set, and I do not want to miss prime hunting time."

"Speak of the devil," I muttered as I wiped the excess ink from Ember's arm. Shade had been the earliest and most vocal witch in the coven to point out my inadequate fire magic. Not that he had any room to talk. He relied on incantations and enchanted artifacts—which he checked out from *my* library—to do his job. I might've been the lamest pyrokinetic in town, but he was the lamest witch all around. I fought the urge to stick my tongue out at him.

Ember pursed her lips, cutting her gaze toward the door he disappeared through before looking at me. "You know what? Why don't you come with us? If we are covered in ghoul guts, it'll be nice for someone else to drive. Congealing innards get sticky fast."

I tugged my dad's Zippo from my pocket and popped open the top. An orange flame grew from the center, flickering in response to my magic. "You want me to go monster hunting with you? I think you've forgotten what happened last time."

Her nostrils flared. There was a reason Ember knew all about ghoul guts, and that reason was me. "You can wait in the car. Be our getaway driver."

"I've been banned from hunting." I touched the flame to the new sigil on her arm, activating it, and the design glowed bright red before fading to a cool blue. The magic would last at least six hours. Once it dissipated, the tattoo would disappear along with her enhanced powers.

She arched a brow, admiring my work. "You're getting really good at this." She tugged her sleeve down. "And you won't be hunting. Just driving."

I laughed dryly. "I don't think the rest of the crew will go for it."

"They won't have a choice. I've made up my mind. You're coming." She rose to her feet and tossed me the keys. "Let's go."

"If you say so." I locked the shop and followed her out the back door. Our black van, complete with magically tinted windows and a hidden arsenal in the floor, sat in the alley behind the eighteenth-century building that had been in my family from the beginning.

The reason Ember was so sure the other witches wouldn't object to my tagging along was that they couldn't. Our parents were the High Priest and Priestess of the Salem order, as were my maternal grandparents and great-grandparents. Being in charge was our birthright, and when Mom and Dad died, the power passed to us.

Well, it passed to our older sister, Cinder. When she went MIA, Ember inherited the torch. And me? I was the introverted librarian tagging along for the ride on my family's coattails.

Actually, that's not fair. I wasn't an introvert. I just

hated people.

A gust of wind whipped through the alley, blowing my hair into my face. Blue strands stuck to my lip gloss, and as I peeled them off and pulled my locks out of my eyes, I found Shade glowering at me.

"Ember...?" His teeth didn't part as he spoke.

My sister smirked and smacked the hood of the van. "Load up. We're burning daylight."

Shade's mouth dropped open. "She's..."

Sis cut him a look that could have melted a glacier in one hot flash. She might have once threatened to roast his chestnuts on an open fire if he ever insulted my magic again, and she probably would have done it. Or at least singed them a bit.

His Adam's apple bobbed, and his right eye twitched. "She's not dressed for hunting."

I crossed my arms over my black corset and shifted my weight to my left leg. Shade wore black spandex pants with a matching shirt. His blond hair was slicked back into a man bun, and a pair of what looked like seatbelt straps crisscrossed his chest, holding a set of wooden stakes.

Chrys, the friendliest witch on the team, wore a similar outfit, though the leggings looked much better on her petite frame. Her chin-length jet-black bob shone in the fading sunlight, and she rolled her eyes, fighting a grin behind his back. Ember and the others wore the same kind of clothes. Take the weapons away, and they all could've been on their way to goth yoga.

"She might snag her tights." Shade crossed his arms to mimic me, so I parked my hands on my hips.

"Fishnets are replaceable. My boot up your ass might be permanent."

"Load. Up." Ember opened the passenger door and cocked her head at me.

"As you wish." This time, I did stick out my tongue.

If Shade glowered any harder, his skull might crack, but he did as he was told and climbed into the van with the others.

I slid into the driver's seat and started the engine. "Where are we headed?"

"The old cemetery outside town. Chrys spotted a few near the mausoleum just before sunrise this morning."

I nodded and reversed out of the alley before hanging a left on Washington. "Let's go kick some vampire butt."

Shade blew a hard breath through his nose, but I ignored him. He was still miffed because I wouldn't go on a second date with him last year. One night with an arrogant prick was more than enough, thank you very much.

The orange sun sank toward the horizon ahead, painting the sky in rich reds and purples. As we approached the top of the hill, the cemetery came into view. Most of the graves had simple headstones, many sinking at awkward angles due to years of neglect, but our target stood near the back fence. The decrepit mausoleum where who knew how many ghouls rested inside.

I pulled as close to the gates as possible, parking sideways so we could make a quick getaway if things got out of hand. Tension built inside the van, making my skin prick. With the sun so low in the sky, the tree's bare branches looked like black bones silhouetted against a watercolor canvas. Spindly fingers stretched across the canopy, their long shadows crisscrossing on the ground like an intricate web.

Leaving the engine running, I turned in my seat to look past the headrest. The witches behind me sat utterly still. Chrys pressed her palms together in prayer to the goddess, while Shade rested the tips of his middle fingers against his thumbs, his lips moving as he silently recited an incantation. Miles and Ginger in the way back seat closed their eyes, either in meditation or prayer. It was hard to tell with those two.

Ember took a deep breath and blew it out, ending her prayer to the goddess. "Everybody ready?"

"Almost," Ginger said.

I pursed my lips, a question forming in my mind. "If vampires fry in the sunlight, why do you wait until dusk to take them out? Seems like you could go in at noon, leave the door open, and stake them all in their sleep."

"Where's the fun in that?" Ember winked before sliding out of the van, and I rolled my eyes. Her life was in peril on a daily basis, and she wouldn't have it any other way. The threat of a mile-high stack of grimoires falling on me was the extent of danger in my life, but someone had to hold down the fort while the big kids played. Lucky me.

Chrys opened the side door, and the rest of the witches filed out of the van. She popped open the secret hatch in the floorboard and pulled out a utility belt with a few knives attached at the hip. The rest of her tools belonged in a garden. She had a spade, a hand-held hoe, and one of those thingamajigs with three claws at the end that was normally used for breaking up dirt. How her gear would help her fight vamps was a mystery to me. Earth witches were weird.

Ember grabbed her enchanted sword, a three-foot-long, solid silver blade with a fireproof rosewood handle and skull pommel. She swiped it through the air as if testing its balance, which was totally unnecessary. She'd had the thing for five years, so she was probably showing off. After twirling it at her side, she gripped it in both hands, blade pointing to the sky. Fire erupted at the hilt, cascading upward until flames engulfed the entire blade.

Yep, definitely showing off.

The rest of the witches pounded pavement toward the gate, but Ember hung back, giving me that supposed-sympathy-but-looked-like-pity expression. "You'll be okay waiting in the van?"

I held up my phone. "I've got three ereader apps and a million books in my TBR. I'll be fine. I might even take a nap."

She nodded and slid the door shut before joining the rest of the crew. They hopped over the waist-high brick fence, not bothering with the gate, and prowled through the cemetery. I could practically hear the dry leaves crunching beneath their boots as they shrank into the darkness and disappeared. Shade's shadow magic came in handy sometimes. I had no problem admitting that, despite his sour demeanor.

While the big kids went off to play with monsters, I clicked my favorite reading app and opened the next installment of the romance series I was addicted to. My goal was to read one hundred novels this year. I still had forty to go and only three months to do it. If these damn monsters would stay on their side of the veil, it would be easy-peasy. With the way things were going lately, I might not make it.

I rolled down the window, stuck my feet through the opening, and sank into my seat, losing myself in the story. Reading had a way of making time stand still and move at warp speed all at once. I wasn't sure how long I'd been sitting there when the shouts echoed from the mausoleum, but it couldn't have been that long. I'd only devoured three chapters.

I snapped my head toward the cemetery, squinting as I peered into the trees. Shade and his damn shadow magic. I couldn't see a thing. I mean, sure, we had to hide ourselves from the humans. If they knew what monsters lurked in the darkness of their quaint little town, all hell would break loose. They'd destroy each other faster than the monsters ever could, so secrecy mattered.

But it didn't stop the irritation bubbling in my gut. I wasn't part of the hunting party, so I was as blind as a human out here in the van.

"Ember!" Chrys screamed, and a flash of firelight illuminated the mausoleum for half a second.

My pulse thrummed, and I sat upright, shoving my phone into the cupholder. Shouting was normal, right? They loved it when the monsters fought back. Danger was wired into their DNA.

The shadows flickered, Shade's magic faltering. That was also normal. Using magic drained us. Even a master witch couldn't hold on to a spell forever.

Another shout. A smack like a body hitting concrete. A pained grunt.

It was the vamps getting their undead asses kicked. Ember was the toughest witch in Salem. She might've been a little reckless, but so were most adrenaline junkies. It was fine. Everything was fine.

Until it wasn't.

The magical shadows rolled toward the mausoleum, billowing at the base of the door before dissipating into the ground. Actually, no. Not the ground. Into Shade. He lay flat on his back, a blood-sucker pinning his shoulders down.

Crap. Where was everyone? Shade was a pain in my rear end, but I didn't want to see him become dinner for the undead.

I opened the door, and my boots thudded on the pavement as I hopped out of the van. My chest burned, my fire magic concentrating in the center of my being. Ember described the sensation as a raging inferno, but to me, it felt like heartburn. The warming sensation spread down my arms until my fingers tingled. My leg muscles tightened, and my stomach clenched as I prepared to sprint into the fray.

But before I could take a step, Ember emerged from the mausoleum, her flame-licked sword swinging through the air and slicing the vampire's head clean off. She kicked the corpse, and it rolled to the ground before melting into goo. After giving Shade a hand up, they both raced back inside.

The final rays of sun disappeared behind the horizon, and I was about to return to the safety of the van and the comfort of my book when movement around the side of the structure caught my eye. A shirtless vampire crept toward a five-foot marble cross, its pale skin gleaming in the moonlight. Dark red blood rimmed its mouth, making my stomach sour. Hopefully the vamp had made a mess of his meal last night, and it wasn't my friend's life force smeared across his face. I held my breath, waiting for a witch to dart out after him, but he kept creeping, and no one noticed.

Well, crapity crap. I couldn't let the monster leave the cemetery. I might have been banned from hunting, but I was still a Veil Keeper, and it was my responsibility to keep the city safe. I chewed my bottom lip, scrunching my nose as the vamp made it halfway to the gate.

I should alert the others, call for Ember or Chrys to come out and nab the bloodsucker. They had the tools and the skills to take it out easily. I had neither. Swallowing the lump in my throat, I forced a scream, "Vamp overboard!"

The commotion inside the mausoleum continued as if I'd only whispered. The vampire, however, heard me just fine. He stopped, tilting his head and looking at me like I was the most delicious slice of blueberry blood pie he'd ever seen. Baring his fangs, he hissed and bolted toward me.

Great plan, Ash. Shouting was definitely the way to go.

My palms tingled, sparks dancing around my

fingertips as I bounced on my toes three times. Then I ran. My boots gripped the pavement, propelling me forward, and thank the goddess, I reached the stone wall before the vamp. I planted one hand on top of the fence, kicking up my legs and clearing it easily. I'd have to send my high school track coach my thanks when this was done.

There were four ways to kill a vampire: sunlight, fire, beheading, and a stake through the heart. Since I didn't have a sword or a UV lamp, my inborn gift of flames would have to do. That and a swift kick to the gut.

I planted my boot in the vamp's stomach, and he stumbled backward into a pile of dead leaves. Rubbing my hands together, I willed the heat to gather in my palms. My fingertips crackled, and as I curled them inward, the sparks ignited.

"Hey, Drac. I've got a kiss for you." I held up my hand and blew on the tiny flame growing from my palm. Fire rolled across my fingers and dropped to the ground a foot shy of my fangy foe. Whoops. I'd been aiming for his pants, but the leaves made perfect fodder for burning him alive...umm...undead.

It hadn't rained in weeks, and the dried shrubbery lit up like a bonfire, taking the vampire with it. He wailed as the flames consumed him, leaving behind nothing of his body but goo and ashes. Enemy number one vanquished. Why was I banned from monster hunting again?

I walked into the fire, being careful not to ruin my boots in the sludge that was once a vampire, and stomped out the flames. Well, my plan was to stomp out the flames. The problem was, they'd already spread out in a four-foot circle and licked upward into a thick spruce. Uh oh.

This was magical fire, though. I should have been able to pull it back inside. To extinguish the flames with my power, just like I'd lit them to begin with. With a deep inhale, I focused again, imagining a cool fog rolling over the flames, putting them out.

The fire grew hotter. The flames jumped from the burning spruce to a maple. You'd think bare branches would take a while to ignite, but no. Magical fire, remember? The inferno jumped from tree to tree, thick gray smoke billowing into the sky.

"Ember..." I backed away from the chaos I'd created before turning on my heel and darting toward the mausoleum. "Ember, I screwed up again!"

My boot caught on an exposed root, and I tumbled toward the entrance, scraping my knees on the concrete. I shot to my feet and launched myself through the door, straight into the path of the last vampire attempting to flee. It smacked into me, our skulls knocking together with a crack before I careened back and it landed on top of me, fangs bared.

I struggled beneath its weight, but it reared back, ready to strike like a viper.

Shade appeared above my head, his face pinched like he'd sucked on a lemon and whiffed a foul fart at the same time. He jabbed a blade into the vamp's back and twisted it before yanking it out. He'd saved my life.

He had not bothered to remove the corpse from atop my body, however. His sour expression turned to one of smugness as the vampire's form melted into a gelatinous mess right on top of me. Cool, sticky goo rolled over me, soaking my corset and making my skin crawl. It smelled of rotten fish and sulfur, and a bit of the nastiness dripped from my cheek backward to my ear.

Covered in ghoul guts. That was what I got for trying to help them.

Ember offered her hand, so I accepted the gesture and let her tug me to my feet. She pointed a finger at the goo on the ground, and a flame shot out, incinerating it. If I wanted to keep my clothes, I'd have to wait until I got home to wash the mess off myself.

"Ash…" Chrys called from the doorway, her voice incredulous. "What did you do?"

"I stopped a vampire from escaping." I followed her out the door to find the entire cemetery engulfed in flames. Heat permeated the threshold like when you first opened an oven door, and the blaze crackled, tree branches snapping and falling to the ground.

"You lit the place on fire." Chrys kneeled, digging her hands into the dirt. She whispered an incantation, and a shockwave extended out in a circle, dirt rising and falling on top of the fire.

Her attempt helped. She extinguished the flames on the ground, but she couldn't do anything about the trees. "Where's a water witch when we need one?" she said as she rose to her feet.

"Can't you call the fire back?" Miles asked.

I held in a dry laugh. He hadn't been in the coven long, but he should have known better. *Everybody* knew better.

"Her magic doesn't work like that," Ember said in my defense.

"It should," I muttered under my breath.

Sirens blasted in the distance, growing louder as they approached, and Ginger jerked her head toward the van. "The humans will handle it. Let's jet."

"Agreed." Ember nodded. "Cloak us, Shade."

The air thickened as the shadow magic activated. Everything took on a grayish tinge, meaning we could see the world but the world couldn't see us. If only I could unsee the vampire guts dripping from my corset.

We ran to the van, Ember heading to the driver's side. I tossed her the keys and opened the passenger door. As I climbed inside, Shade stopped beside me and eyed my bloodied knees.

"I told you you'd snag your tights." He smirked and crawled into the back seat.

I hated it when he was right.

TWO

"Good morning, sunshine." Ember gave me a tentative smile and gestured to the wad of black plastic in my hand. "What's in the bag?"

"What's left of my corset. I didn't get the ghoul guts off in time, and it ate a hole through the lining." I clutched the bag and brushed past her in the narrow hallway. Damn vampires needed to stay in the spirit realm where they belonged. There were plenty of reasons ghosts, ghouls, and faeries lived in another dimension, and toxic innards were near the top of the list.

"I'll get you a new one on my way home from work." She followed behind me, matching my pace as I went down the stairs and out the back door.

"No need. I've got plenty." I tossed the bag into the

dumpster and gestured to the corset I had on. They really weren't as uncomfortable as people made them out to be. Plus, I had a tendency to slump, and the snug fit reminded me to stand up straight and be the proud elemental witch I was. Ha.

Ember twirled her keys around her finger before clutching them in her hand. "Yeah, but it's my fault you were at the cemetery last night."

"And it's my fault for trying to use my defective fire magic and burning the place to the ground."

A familiar look of pity pinched her features, so I shook my head and said, "I'm a librarian and sigil artist. I should know better by now."

She shifted her weight to her right leg. "You were tired. Five sigils in a row would have taken a toll on Dad too. I bet if you'd had time to recover properly, you would have—"

"I wouldn't."

"You might have..."

I sighed and tilted my head. I knew my place, and I should have stayed in it.

She glanced at her phone and held the screen toward me. "The humans put out the fire. At least now they might do some upkeep on the place, take care of the graves."

"Mm-hmm." I stood in the doorway, leaning my shoulder against the jamb.

Ember returned her phone to her pocket. "I'm

heading to work. Want to grab dinner at Rockafellas when I get home?"

"Sure." I waved as she climbed into her black Jeep and drove away.

Ember worked at Spellbound Axe, which was perfect for her. She got paid to teach people how to throw sharp objects. Being the coven librarian was a full-time job—the perfect job for me—so membership dues paid my salary. With my home upstairs and the library and shop downstairs, I rarely left the building. Last night was a reminder why.

Before I could spin the disco ball at my pity party for one, I locked the back door and headed for the library. My Mary Janes thudded on the hardwood as I stepped into my sanctuary and took a deep breath. The musty smell of old books filled my senses, relaxing the tension in my shoulders. I rolled my neck and inhaled again.

Ahhh… This was where I belonged.

To the right lay the arsenal. Dozens upon dozens of magical artifacts sat on the wooden shelves, each one labeled with its purpose, instructions, and remedy. I had created the laminated cards for the items because a couple of inexperienced witches botched the spells a while ago.

People weren't supposed to check out items unless they'd done their research and knew how to use them, but when a seventeen-year-old, who was trying to cure his genital warts with magic, came running in with boils covering his entire body, I had to drop everything and look up a spell to reverse the hex he'd cast on himself. I wasn't a healer by any means, but research was my department, so I helped him.

Of course, I told him to see a real doctor for his problem. Magic couldn't fix everything, and a warty wiener was better than puss-filled boils any day of the week.

So, every artifact now came with instructions, thanks to me. That project was complete, so it was time to organize the grimoires.

I hit the switch on the wall, and the overhead lights hummed to life, casting a dim, warm glow on the tomes. Wooden cabinets lined the other three walls, while six rows of shelves stood in the center of the room. Ancient texts stood next to new editions, and stacks of books that needed to be reshelved sat in the aisles, making it nearly impossible to find anything.

When my dad ran the library, he'd locate the books by sense. If he closed his eyes and said a location spell, his magic would lead him to the volume he needed. I could do that too, but it would be a helluva lot easier if they were organized. The Dewey Decimal System was still in use for a reason.

It worked.

I started with the sigil books, since those were the

most familiar. I'd studied them from cover to cover when I was training to be Ink Master, and though I rarely needed to crack one open anymore, they were my favorite. Embossed sigils adorned the deep burgundy covers, and as I ran my fingers over the first volume, magic tingled on my skin.

I set it on the shelf nearest my desk and picked up the next one on the stack, volume three. Where was two? The books left in the pile were volumes six, four, eight, seven, and nine, in that order. I couldn't very well organize them if I didn't have all the books, so I scanned the cabinets along the wall, looking for the burgundy cover. Nothing.

Creeping down the aisle between the piles of books, I searched and searched. A thick layer of dust coated the shelves and everything on them. It looked like I'd be getting after the entire room with a feather duster soon.

The next aisle of books was even worse. Volumes thrown haphazardly on the shelves created a chaos that made my muscles crawl beneath my skin. It would take weeks to organize this mayhem, and if I didn't find sigil book two, I'd never sleep at night. Looked like it was time to use magic.

Straightening my shoulders, I tipped my head toward the sky...I mean ceiling...and called on my magic. "What was lost will be found. Near or far, show me where you are."

The vibrating energy in the room stilled, leaving only a faint tickle above my head. That was weird. If the book were in the library, I would have been pulled right to it. Instead, the weak vibration came from far away...as in upstairs. What was it doing up there? I hadn't cracked open a sigil book in ages, so it couldn't be in my room.

I ground my teeth. "Ember..."

Why on earth would she be studying sigils? Wasn't it enough that she was good at *everything* else? Sigils were supposed to be my thing.

I stomped out of the library, up the stairs, and through the kitchen. She'd left her cereal bowl in the sink again, which made my irritation with her double. When I reached the hallway, I expected the vibration to pull me into the first bedroom, Ember's. Instead, it led me farther down, past my room, and toward Cinder's.

Okay, that was weird. Cinder always made a big deal out of me and my ink, so I couldn't fathom why she'd be studying them. Leave it to the oldest to coddle the youngest, right? Honestly, I appreciated her encouragement more than she knew.

I hesitated in the doorway. I hadn't set foot inside her room since she disappeared. Ember had gone in, looking for clues as to where she might have gone, but she'd found nothing. No notes scribbled on scraps of paper. No maps to her location. Nada.

With a deep inhale, I crossed the threshold. The moment I stepped inside, the sigil book's vibration stilled. I whispered the location spell again, but nothing happened.

"Huh." I took a giant step backward, into the hallway, and poof. The magic took hold, pulling me back into Cinder's room. "Strange."

Poof again. The book's vibration stopped the second I crossed the threshold.

"What have you been up to, big sister?" I straightened my shoulders. Time to find out exactly what she'd done. "Confess, expose my magic sleuth. I call on you to reveal your truth."

Golden sparkles gathered in the air, revealing a thick gray cloud billowing from the ceiling, stretching down and engulfing the entire space. She'd cast a cloaking spell to hide something, and unless I removed it, my location magic would be useless in her room.

I stepped out and ran to the kitchen to mix up a quick potion. Solomon's seal, star anise, and a pinch of basil formed the base of my spell. I mixed everything together, and as I added a drop of lavender oil, pink smoke rose from the bowl, the mixture turning into a fine powder.

Back in Cinder's room, I blew the dust into the air and said, "Magic cloak, I now revoke."

The moment the final word crossed my lips,

Cinder's spell fought back, slapping me across the face like a scorned lover. The gray cloud thickened, swirling around me and making my skin sting. I made the mistake of breathing it in. My nostrils burned as if my dear, sweet oldest sister had shot a stream of fire from her fingertips straight up my nose.

I coughed and stumbled back into the hall. "What the actual eff, Cin?"

Why would she need a spell that strong in her bedroom? All I wanted was to find sigil book volume two, but apparently, even in her absence...or her death—I wasn't ruling it out yet—Cinder thought that was too much to ask.

Shaking off the essence of her uber-mega-ridiculously-too-strong-spell—what was she hiding?—I crossed the threshold for the fourth, and hopefully final, time. I'd have to find the book the mortal way.

A quick scan of her bookcase revealed nothing of use. A high school yearbook, a few horror novels, a figurine of a black cat dressed like a reaper. Her nightstand stood empty on top. I was afraid of what I might find in the drawer, but I had to look.

My lip curled. Great. Now I'd seen my sister's vibrator, a hot pink number with a little tail sticking out the front...or maybe it was for the back? Either way, it was a sight I couldn't unsee.

"Why are you making this so hard, Cinder?"

I went for the underwear drawer next. I'd already

seen what she put inside her hoo-ha, so I might as well rummage through what she covered it with. Black lace and pink satin. Nothing kinky, thank the goddess. Also, no book. I didn't find it any of her drawers, so I moved on to the closet.

Shoving her shirts aside, I fumbled through the small space. Every pair of shoes, minus the ones she had on when she went MIA, sat in an orderly fashion along the wall. She had a few boxes on the shelf above the hangers, but none were big enough to hold the tome I was searching for.

I dropped to the floor, my knees thudding on the wood. I didn't have a clue why she had felt the need to hide my book, but my irritation tipped to frustration. Next would come anger, and I refused to be mad at a dead woman. *Possibly dead*, I corrected myself.

"Seriously, Cin. What else are you hiding?" I felt along the baseboards, searching for a secret panel in the wall or the floor. Yes, Ember rummaged through her room when she first went missing, but my middle sister wasn't the greatest at attention to detail. She'd told me she checked for hidey holes, and I'd taken her word for it so I wouldn't have to come into this room and deal with the emotions it might dredge up.

I missed the heck out of Cinder. My parents too. But I refused to get all blubbery over it again. Tears wouldn't bring them back. Actions might, but so far, none of our attempts had done a lick of good.

We'd tried scrying, location spells, talking to everyone who knew her, even in passing. Nothing. It was like she'd dropped off the face of the earth. We'd even filed a missing person report with the human police. She either didn't want to be found or she really had disintegrated into the ether. That or she somehow got sucked through to the other side of the veil, and if that were the case, she was as good as gone forever.

Anyway, I'd managed to keep the feels in check thus far. No need to go slogging down memory lane now.

I followed the floorboards around the entire room and didn't find any panels. Ember had done a good job after all. A sweep of my phone's flashlight beneath the bed revealed nothing but a few dust bunnies. No latches. No disturbances in the wood. That left one place Ember might have missed.

Rising to my feet, I tugged on the mattress, but it didn't budge. Weird. It wasn't some ultra-thick support mattress. I should have been able to at least slide it to the side, but it was stuck. Magically stuck.

"Cinder, Cinder. I've found your secret stash, haven't I?" I hovered my hands above the sheets, and sure enough, magic tingled on my palms. A simple weight spell held the mattress in place, or so I assumed. The cloaking spell masked the true magic, so she must've counted on that to do all the work. This weight spell was Witchy 101 stuff. I didn't even need a potion to cancel it, as long as she hadn't ampli-fied it to fight back. Surely she wouldn't do that to me twice.

"Light as a feather, soft as down, I turn this spell right around." The air thickened and then popped, releasing the pressure as the charm disintegrated.

My stomach tightened as my fingers slid beneath the mattress. Lifting it was a breeze without the spell in place, and lo and behold, there on the boxed springs sat volume two of my sigil collection. Next to it lay a leather-bound book with the Tree of Life debossed on the cover. A piece of brown twine wrapped around it, securing the pages closed.

I grabbed them both before letting the mattress fall back into place. Why in the goddess's name would she hide this volume? Or better yet, *who* was she hiding it from?

Not me. I'd memorized every sigil in this book years ago, and Ember couldn't be bothered to learn them. I pursed my lips, my gaze shifting from my book to the leather one.

"Ugh. Whatever." I had it back, and that was what mattered. Now I could get on with the cataloging I should have done a month ago.

I pulled the door shut behind me and made my way downstairs to the library, where I dropped into my chair and laid the books on the desk. The leather one I had never seen before, so I untied the twine and opened it to what should have been the title page. But this wasn't a book. It was a diary.

Cinder's diary.

I slammed it shut and fumbled with the twine. Once I secured it, I slid it into the drawer and rested my elbows on the desk, pressing my fingers to my temples. I didn't keep a diary myself. My innermost thoughts were best left deep in the recesses of my mind, and my sister's needed to remain in hers.

Eyeing the journal in the open drawer, I chewed my bottom lip. It was tempting, I'd give it that, and if I were ten years younger, I would have dived right in. At twenty-four, I could control my urges now...most of the time.

I shoved it closed and picked up the sigil volume, fanning through the pages. As I rose to place it on the shelf, a thick piece of yellowing parchment drifted to the floor. Huh. This book was old, but not *that* old. The pages had just begun to turn around the edges. The loose one could've been printed a few hundred years ago.

I snatched it up and sank into my chair before turning on the desk lamp. My pulse sprinted as I unfolded it and found a set of three sigils I had never seen before. Centered down the middle of the page, the symbols appeared hand drawn. The patterns of the ink indicated the artist had used a quill rather than a pen. Intricate arrays of curved and straight lines crisscrossed and coiled into elaborate designs no amateur could accomplish with a tattoo machine. These were graduate-level sigils, if I'd ever seen any.

The only other writing on the page was a single word beneath each design:

Chaos.

Mayhem.

Discord.

"What the ever-loving...?" I traced my finger over the top design. The coarseness of the paper felt rough against my skin. "Where did you get this, Cin?"

The back of the page was blank. No header or footer or even a page number to give a clue as to where it came from. A black magic tome, possibly? Maybe, but no sinister vibrations emanated from the page. I couldn't feel any magic at all. Could Cinder have neutralized it?

I wasn't sure, but curiosity had me itching to try one out. Power over chaos? Yes, please. With a snap of my fingers, I could have the library organized and cataloged in an instant. Maybe then I could catch up on my reading goal.

Long strides carried me out of the library toward the front of the building. My tattoo machine sat on its stand, a fresh supply of ink on the shelf above it. I set the parchment on the table, but I hesitated to set up the device.

My dad had warned me never to try a new sigil

alone, and he was talking about the ones from our collection. Without knowing where this one came from, I had no clue how my body would react if I did it wrong.

But when was the last time I'd messed up a sigil—besides protection, which was the trickiest one? Years ago, at least. I was well on my way to becoming an Ink Master if I still had a master to train under.

I crossed my arms, tapping my foot as I stared at the page. Ember would be gone for hours. My inbox was empty, which meant no one had leads on any new disturbances in the veil. The coven wouldn't need me for a while, and if anyone botched a spell, they could see our resident healer, Patrice.

The front door was still locked. I had an hour before the tourist shop was supposed to open. A smile tugged at my lips. "Let's do this."

Was it reckless? Probably, but Ember didn't own the market on heedless decisions. Bookish girls could be rebellious too.

Besides, our lives had been total chaos for six months, first with my parents' deaths and then with Cinder's disappearance. A little control over the uncontrollable would be welcomed by us all.

I practiced first with pen and paper, gently tracing the design to get a feel for the dips and curves. Sigil tattoos had to be drawn freehand for the magic to work, so I drew it on another sheet and compared the two. It was as perfect a match as could be. Easy peasy. I had this.

With my mind made up, I poured the magical ink into my favorite well and rolled up my sleeve. If this sigil lasted the full six hours, imagine what I could get done. Excitement bubbled in my stomach as I attached the needle and turned on the machine.

The first curve of the design hurt like a bitch. The skin on the inside of the wrist was thin, which made it a painful place for tattoos. Chaos's symbol was long, though, so I needed my entire forearm to make sure I got the proportions right.

I winced with the next line. I'd forgotten just how painful these could be. The third line extended up my arm, almost to my elbow, before bending down and swirling a bit like a treble clef. Deep breath in. Long exhale. The needle pulsed in and out of my skin so rapidly that the noise sounded like a vibration.

Sharp pain in my temple told me I was clenching my teeth, so I relaxed my jaw and put the final swoop on the design. My entire body tingled. Both channeling magic and receiving it felt like the kind of adrenaline rush you'd get before skydiving. Or so I imagined. You'd never see me jumping out of a perfectly good airplane on purpose.

With the machine back on its rack, I held up my arm to admire my work. It looked exactly like the original. Time to light this baby up.

I reached into my pocket for the Zippo, but my hand met an empty pouch of fabric. I patted down my jeans, but the familiar metal rectangle didn't protrude from any of my pockets. Crappity crap. I must've left it in my room.

Call me lazy, but I did not feel like traipsing all the way back upstairs to get it. Ember would tell me to use my fire magic. A little spark was all I needed to activate the sigil. If I had drawn this on anyone else, I wouldn't dare. One little flash from me would likely go haywire and singe someone's eyebrows.

A new sigil on myself, though... Why the hell not?

I rubbed the tips of my fingers against my thumb, charging up my magic. My palm pricked with energy, and I focused it into my index finger before pointing it at my arm. Heat rolled from my chest outward until a tiny flame shot out, lighting the design on fire.

It glowed bright crimson like it was supposed to, but as the flames subsided, it didn't fade to cool blue. The sigil remained red, undulating like hot magma flowing through a tunnel.

Uh oh. That didn't look good.

Nausea churned in my stomach, and my breakfast threatened to make a reappearance. My head spun. I squeezed my eyes shut and waited for the dizzying sensation to pass. A garbled roar sounded from somewhere outside, but I couldn't be bothered to look out the window. I was too busy trying to keep from passing out.

"Ouch. Son of a bitch." I clutched my head, applying pressure to counter the skull-splitting sensation.

The garbled roar grew louder. *"Who dares summon Chaos?"*

Seriously? Was another tour guide going off-script? Our city was so rich in history and horror, yet some tour companies always felt the need to embellish the truth for better ratings.

Wait. Did he say...chaos? The sigil on my arm pulsed. Nah, that would be too much of a coincidence. Still...

I stumbled to the window to get a look at the culprit, but the street lay empty. Not a soul in sight. The roar filled my head, nearly bursting my eardrums. *"Answer me!"*

My stomach lurched. I barely made it to the trash can in time to stop the partially digested fruity cereal from spilling all over the floor. I heaved again, and again the voice roared.

Holy mother of the devil himself. That raspy, roaring voice hadn't come from outside. It had come from inside.

Inside *me*.

CHAPTER
THREE

I swear my brain rattled in my skull; the voice shook me so hard. My stomach was finally empty, though, so that was a plus. Pressing the heels of my hands against my temples, I stumbled to my feet. A growl rumbled between my ears. What the hell had I just done?

The page of sigils lay on the counter, so I grabbed it and paced to the library. This headache was bad enough to unalive me. Hopefully it wouldn't hinder my magic before I found a cure. I had to find the book of healing spells before I passed out from the pain. If the library was organized like it was supposed to be, I could open a drawer, find the little card for the book I needed, and know exactly where it was. Or, if it was organized like the plans I had for it, I could type *spell to relieve headaches* into the computer, and I'd get a list of possibilities with their locations in the stacks.

Instead, I had to use a location spell. A spell to find a freaking spell.

"Release me, witch," the rumbling voice demanded.

"Believe me, buddy. As soon as I figure out how, I will." I closed my eyes and took a deep breath, preparing for the incantation.

"Release me now! Where is my skull?" he screamed and then roared so loud my entire body shook.

"I don't have your skull, but you're about to crack mine." I clutched my head, my nostrils flaring as I blew out a breath. "Listen, man...or monster. Whatever you are, if you don't quiet down, I'm going to black out. Then I won't be able to help either of us. I have to fix me before I can figure out how to fix you, so shut the eff up for a minute, okay?"

He growled at a tolerable level this time.

"What was lost will be found. Near or far, show me where you are." I'd done this spell so many times I didn't need a potion to activate it. The book tugged me toward it, and relief flooded my veins. I grabbed the volume from the shelf and returned to my desk to find headaches in the index. The pages rustled as I flipped to the spell.

"Thank the goddess." It was a simple one. No potion required for this one, either. "May the light of the goddess lift my pain. My headache will ease like a cleansing rain."

The splitting agony reduced to a dull ache, and I could finally think. Holy mother of magic. I had a voice inside my head, and it wasn't the running dialog I constantly had with myself. My forearm throbbed, and I laid it on the table to find the sigil pulsing red.

"That is my mark."

The pain in my head intensified, making me wince. "I need you to use your inside voice. You know...since you're *inside* my head."

"Why is my mark on your person?"

My person? Who talked like that? Better question... "Who are you?"

"I am Chaos—" he started to boom.

I clutched my head again. "If that's your inside voice, then you need to whisper. Seriously."

A soft growl rumbled between my ears. *"I am Chaos, Prince of Hell. Why did you summon me?"*

"Prince of..." A maniacal giggle bubbled from my throat. No way. I had not done what I thought I'd just done. "You're..." I bit my lip. "You're saying you're a demon?"

"A Prince of Hell."

"Which is a demon." I picked up the page of sigils. *Demonic* sigils. Oof.

"I am no simple fiend. I am of the highest level in Hell, a commander of armies, a destroyer of all who vex me."

"Right, but you're still a demon. I mean, all the creatures of Hell are some sort of demon, princes included. Is that correct?"

He grunted, clearly displeased with my assessment. *"Yes."*

"Great. Now we're getting somewhere. You're a demon prince, and you're inside my head. Want to tell me how you got there?" Because the only sigil I had ever flubbed was Cinder's protection tattoo.

I laid my arm next to the design on the paper. It was a perfect match, so there had to be another reason why, instead of harnessing power over chaos, I'd invited *Chaos* to take up space in my head.

"How did you summon me from my imprisonment?"

Fantabulous. Not only had I possessed myself with a demon prince, but I'd nabbed one straight from his prison cell. He must've been a bad, bad boy. "Who threw you in the brig? Lucifer himself, Hades, or do you report to someone in the middle?"

"How did you summon me, witch?"

I blew out an exasperated breath. "We aren't getting anywhere ignoring each other's questions. First off, I have a name. It's Ash, and I want you to use it. You say witch like it's a bad thing to be."

"It's an abominable thing to be!"

"You think so, eh? And demons are soooo nice to be around." Frakity frak. This guy had to go. Rather than sitting around and arguing with the voice in my head, I should be finding a spell to kick him to the curb. What volume would have the steps to perform an exorcism?

My own growl rumbled in my throat as I slammed the healing book shut and focused my energy. "What was lost will be found. Near or far, show me where you are. Exorcisms."

"What are you doing, wi...Ash? You cannot exorcise a Prince of Hell. Not without my skull."

"Watch me." I rummaged through the stack of books where I felt the magic pull me, but the one the spell had led me to was for exiling fae back across the veil. Still, I flipped through the pages in hopes it had a chapter on demons. The most useful thing I found was a healing salve to spread over a faery bite. Those nasty little suckers had mouths full of razors. Tinkerbells they were not.

I cast the location spell again, this time making sure to focus on demon exorcisms. A crooked stack of books stood in front of me, threatening to tumble to the floor, but I couldn't be bothered with it. I tiptoed around it, swinging my hips away from the pile to avoid giving it any incentive, and made my way to the back of the room.

The overhead lights barely illuminated this part of the library, so I relied on the magic to guide me to the right book. Covered with black leather, the tome vibrated in my hands as I picked it up and carried it back to my desk. An embossed pentagram took up most of the front cover, and the spine creaked when I opened it.

Fabulous. It was written entirely in Latin.

I whipped out my trusty cell phone and opened the translate app. Hovering the camera over the first page, I let it do its thing. You'd think, with how advanced AI was and all, that someone would have invented a spell-casting app by now. Just tell the software what you wanted to do, and it would scan all the documents on the witchy web and find you the perfect incantation.

Maybe I'd work on that after I organized the coven library. One thing at a time, Ash, and right now, I needed to get Chaos out of my head.

"Your attempts will be futile." At least he'd learned to modulate his volume. *"No simple witch can banish me."*

"I'm no simple witch." Now it was my turn to boast. "I'm Ash Holland, as in the Holland witches of Salem. Direct descendent of the first High Priestess on this continent. The women in my family are so important, the men take *our* last name." Not that I was all that important myself, but our lineage sure as hell was.

"A Holland witch," he grumbled.

"Damn straight. Now that you know who you're dealing with, zip it so I can send you on your way, mm-kay?"

He responded with silence. Halleluiah.

With the help of the translation app, I found an incantation for banishing a demon across the veil. It wasn't *exactly* an exorcism, but it was close enough. I hoped. The translator was far from perfect, but I knew enough Latin to get the gist of what this spell would do. Honestly, I didn't care where it sent Chaos, as long as he vacated my head.

Closing my eyes, I centered myself. "Goddess, please assist me in banishing this demon. As I will it, so mote it be."

Magic tingled in my stomach, working its way up to my chest. I lit the appropriately colored candles and smudged the four corners of the room with white sage.

"That scent is atrocious."

"Of course it is to you, *demon*." I dripped as much disdain from the last word as my current state of focus would allow. "Now shut it."

Tracing my finger along the words, I recited the incantation, doing my absolute best to pronounce the syllables right. A long E spoken with a short sound could be the difference between banishing this creature and turning my beautiful blue locks into swamp moss.

Yes, I knew that from experience.

When I'd uttered the final word, I closed my eyes, inhaling deeply and bracing myself for whatever it felt like to have a demon forcibly removed from your body. I'd seen plenty of movies about it, but I highly doubted it would be as painful as if a Catholic priest were in charge. Witches did everything with more finesse.

So much more finesse, in fact, that I didn't even feel the creature leave my body. "Huh. That didn't hurt at all."

"That is because I'm still here."

"Well, crap."

"I told you it wouldn't work. You cannot remove me from your person without my skull in your possession. You should not have been able to summon me without it."

I dropped into my seat, the chair creaking as it absorbed my weight. Looked like a squirt of WD-40 was in order for this thing. Hey, witches didn't use magic for everything. We'd exhaust ourselves with menial tasks and have nothing left for the important stuff like monster hunting...and book cataloging.

Flipping through the pages of this ancient text, I scanned the Latin with my phone, hoping to find a more specific exorcism spell. No luck.

"Why is my mark on your person?" Chaos asked, his voice dripping with annoyance.

I was the one with a demon knocking around

inside my skull. If anyone should be annoyed, it was me. Then again, he didn't possess me on purpose. Maybe a little communication with the beast wouldn't hurt.

"Most draw a demon's mark on the ground inside a sacred circle before summoning him."

"Yeah, well, I didn't know these were demon-summoning symbols. We're a light coven; dark magic is forbidden. I thought I was going to harness power over chaos and organize my library."

A deep chuckle reverberated in my chest, but it didn't come from me. *"You summoned a Prince of Hell for organizational reasons?"*

"You don't listen very well. I just said I didn't know these were demon marks." Wait. Was he listening to my actual voice, or could he read my thoughts? Maybe I was wasting my breath. *"Can you hear me now? Can you read my mind?"*

"You are an Ink Master. That explains your ability to draw me from my prison."

"I'm not an Ink Master." I waited for a response, giving him more than a beat or two to reply to my argument. When he didn't, I figured he couldn't actually read my mind. "My dad was the Ink Master. I'm just the apprentice."

"Self-deprecation is rarely a quality in a witch with your level of power. You are an Ink Master. You would not

have been able to summon me into your person otherwise. Or did your father summon me, using you as a vessel?"

My nose scrunched involuntarily. "Will you stop calling my body my 'person'? It's weird. And I am not a vessel. My dad is dead. I did this. I will fix it."

"You are the Ink Master and a fire witch. The most powerful Veil Keeper in Salem."

I snorted. "Hardly."

"It's the truth."

"Sure." I couldn't stop the laugh rolling up from my belly if I tried. "You're a funny little demon."

"You have no concept of my size. I am a mighty warrior." His voice increased a few decibels with each word.

"What did I tell you about inside voices? Anyway, like I said, I'm just the apprentice."

"An apprentice operates under the supervision of a master. Is there another of that level besides your father?"

I shrugged. "Nope. It's just me now."

"Are there other ink witches in your coven?"

"I'm the only one."

"Then you are the master."

"Okay. Fine." I threw up my hands. "You can call me the Ink Master if that will make you happy."

"The only thing that would make me happy would be for you to remove me from your person."

"And to do that, I need your skull, right?"

"Correct."

"Perfect. So I'll fetch your severed head, perform another banishing spell, and then you can be on your way. Where can I find your skull?"

His growl rumbled in my chest. *"I do not know."*

CHAPTER

FOUR

"What do you mean, you don't know?" I shot to my feet and paced to the front of the shop. In my excitement about harnessing power over chaos and then the detriment of my possessing myself with *Chaos*, I never opened the store.

"*I am not aware of my skull's current location.*" Chaos grunted like he was annoyed again.

"I understood what you said, doofus. I mean, *why* don't you know?"

"*That is not what you asked.*"

"Well, it's what I meant." I turned the Closed sign over to Open and disengaged the lock. Since our building was on the edge of downtown, we had to keep up appearances. Our mom had converted the front quarter of the downstairs into a witchy shop—

one of the bajillion already in Salem. We offered smudge sticks, candles, spell kits, and other souvenirs for the tourists and local people who practiced witchcraft but didn't possess any real magic.

"I have been trapped in darkness across the veil since the witch who vanquished my brothers and me bound us. I have no knowledge of where she placed our skulls. Without them, we cannot resurrect."

"No wonder you don't like witches. I mean, the realm across the veil is nasty enough, but to be imprisoned in darkness there? Yuck."

The bell above the door chimed, and a pair of women in black jackets and witch hats—one purple, one green—scurried in. The quickest way to stand out as a tourist in Salem was to wear a witch hat, but I wasn't about to tell them that. Tourism made up a huge chunk of the city's revenue, and the money we made from our little storefront paid the taxes on the building.

"Welcome to the Holland Witchery." I plastered on my salesperson's smile and gave a little wave.

"Hi." Purple Hat returned the gesture, but Green had already picked up a love spell kit in one hand and a heart-mending spell in the other. An interesting decision was about to be made.

"How long have I been imprisoned that witches can walk freely amongst mortals?"

I let out a huff of laughter. "Those aren't witches."

Green's head snapped toward me. "What?"

"Umm... Oh, I said 'Those aren't the right stitches.' I was talking to myself. I used the wrong stitches on this corset." Running my finger along the seam, I drew her attention toward the fabric and away from my rude comment. The last thing I needed to do was insult the customers.

"Are you a real witch?" Purple approached the counter with a smudge stick in her hand. "Do these really work?"

"Witches who cannot recognize their brethren?"

I cleared my throat. "It depends on what you're using it for, but yes. Sage helps to cleanse negative energy from a space."

She grabbed three more sticks from the bin and laid them on the counter.

Green Hat put the heart-mending spell back on the rack and brought the love spell to the register. I held in a chuckle. If she planned to make whoever hurt her fall in love, she would be sorely disappointed. Our magic never interfered with free will, and the spell kits we sold didn't do much more than help the mundane focus their intentions.

"What century is this?"

"It's the twenty-first."

"What is?" Purple tilted her head, looking at me quizzically.

Crap. If I kept talking to Chaos like everyone else

could hear him, I'd be on the fast track to the looney bin. I grabbed the spell kit and scanned the barcode. "This is the twenty-first love spell we've sold this week. Must be in the air." I waved my hands, wiggling my fingers to indicate magic.

"Must be." Purple cut a sideways glance at Green, clearly disapproving of her choice. The women turned to leave, and the bell chimed again as Ember strode through the door.

"We've got a case..." She froze and flicked her gaze toward the customers. "...of smudge sticks in the back. Can you help me?"

Purple and Green scurried on to the next shop while Em locked the door behind them.

"Nice save." I strode to the entrance and flipped the Open sign to Closed. "What's up?"

"You are supposed to be retrieving my skull, not selling trinkets to humans playing at magic."

I gritted my teeth. No way in all the Underworld could I let my sister know how badly I'd screwed up this time, which meant *not* answering the disembodied voice. Light witches were forbidden from summoning demons, and especially from trapping them inside their own bodies.

"I demand you release me."

I raised a finger toward my sister. "Hold that thought. I need to pee, and then you can tell me all about it."

Ember huffed. "Hurry. I took off work for this. The police chief is waiting for us."

"'Kay." I scurried around the counter.

She followed me into the back, through the sigil area, and into the library, where I was planning to have a pointed conversation with the demon in my head.

"Actually, I think it might be number two. I'm going to head upstairs for some privacy, if you don't mind. That breakfast burrito I had this morning isn't agreeing with me."

"I thought you had cereal." She plopped into the squeaky chair at my desk, making a face as it groaned.

"I had the burrito after you left. Be right back." I darted up the stairs before she could say anything else. Rounding the corner, I paced down the hall and ducked into the bathroom. After turning on the extraction fan and running the water, I fisted my hands.

"Listen, Chaos. Since you can't release yourself, I don't think you're in any position to be demanding stuff from me. My coven and I are the supernatural police of Salem. A select few humans in high positions of authority know about us, and if they ask for our help, it's because something bad happened and they suspect magic was involved. The veil is thinner here in Salem than anywhere else."

He had the nerve to growl after my speech. *"I am*

aware of the magical nature of this town. I was summoned here long before you came into existence."

"Good. Then you understand the kind of shit that can go down here. We just took out a nest of vamp ghouls who'd somehow made it to this side, so there is no telling what's going on now."

"Locating my skull is the first step to solving your problems."

I scoffed. "You have no idea the scope of my problems right now. My sister is the acting High Priestess. She absolutely cannot find out I summoned you."

"Perhaps she could be of assistance."

"Nope. No way. I made this mess; I'll clean it up. But first I have to deal with the humans' problem. Once that's done, I'll find your skull. I need you to keep quiet while I'm around Ember. We could be looking at mutiny if the coven found out I was consorting with a demon."

Ember rapped her knuckles on the door. "You okay in there?"

I flushed and whispered, "Please be quiet."

His growl reverberated through my entire body. *"Very well."*

After shutting off the water and the extraction fan, I sprayed some air freshener to cover up the fact I had not stunk up the place and plastered on a smile as I opened the door. "All better." I linked my arm around

Ember's and guided her away from the bathroom. "What's going on?"

Her boots clunked on the wood as we descended the narrow staircase. "A group of teens has gone missing from the woods. One made it out and swears a monster took his friends."

Chaos rumbled inside me, so I cleared my throat, stopping him from speaking. "A monster, eh? Did he get a good look at it?"

Ember stopped at the bottom of the stairs, resting one hand on her hip. "Cracked skin the color of partially burned charcoal."

The skin around my eyes scrunched as I tried to imagine the description. "So like black and gray?"

She nodded. "With curly horns coming out of its forehead."

"That's a demon. Lower-mid-level. Still not capable of maintaining a human form."

My mouth pinched, and I cleared my throat, but Chaos didn't take the hint.

"The skin looks like charcoal because it is burnt. It will flake and rain down around it as it moves, scorching the earth."

"Whoa." I pinched the bridge of my nose and squeezed my eyes shut. That was not good.

"Are you okay?" Ember rested a hand on my shoulder.

"Yeah. Just a lingering headache from yesterday. It

sounds like someone summoned a demon. You don't think they were coven members, do you?"

"They'd better not be. With all the shit that's gone down in the past few months, a power grab wouldn't surprise me, though. I've heard rumblings about my lack of leadership skills."

My empty stomach suddenly felt like a brick dropped into it. Why hadn't the idea crossed my mind before? "Wait. Do you think Mom, Dad, and Cinder... Do you think someone's picking us off one by one? Do we have a traitor in the coven?"

"No. No way. They might submit a vote of no confidence to the Higher Power, but they wouldn't use violence or kidnapping." Her words may have said that, but the tightness around her eyes and mouth said she wasn't so sure.

"Mutiny is already abound."

"No, it's not." I stomped toward my tattoo machine.

"What's not?" Ember followed.

Crap. Can it, Chaos. "It's not a coven member. They wouldn't dare. So, what do you want then? If I could figure out a way to make speed and strength permanent on you, it would save us a ton of time."

"I need you to come with me and check it out."

I laughed. "You've got a short memory, don't you?"

"It's not an active scene. Whatever took those kids...*if* anything took them at all...is long gone. Hell, the boy could have been tripping on acid and imagined the whole thing."

"Let's hope." I crossed my arms and worried my lower lip between my teeth. It sure would have been handy if Chaos could read my thoughts. I had so many questions. "I'm still not sure I should go. What if something is still there? I could burn the forest down if I had to fight."

"Nothing is there. The humans have been there for two hours already. If a demon wanted to take someone else, he'd grab a mundane before he'd mess with a witch."

"Unless he had a vendetta against witches."

I scoffed. "Like you?"

"Or like you," Ember replied, though my comment was directed at Chaos. "You're the best at reading spells. I need you to figure out what, if any, magic was used so we can locate the missing kids."

"If they're really missing."

"Exactly."

"All right. I can handle that, but if a hungry beastie pops up, that's all you."

She grinned. "Deal."

"I don't like this." I slid out of the van and slammed the door before pacing around to the driver's side. Ember wasn't packing her sword, nor did she let me arm her with sigils. "What if something happens? What if it's a trap?"

Her brows shot toward her hairline before she recovered. "It's fine. Look, Chief Higgins is right over there, and his gun is holstered. If there was a threat, he wouldn't be chewing on a toothpick with his hands on his hips."

I crossed my arms. "He'd be blind to a magical threat."

She waved a hand dismissively. "It'll be fine. Here." She slid open the side door and retrieved her sword from the secret compartment in the floorboard before laying it across the back seat. "It's ready if I need it. I'll take care of you, little sister."

It wasn't me I was worried about. I had no problem turning tail and running if things went south. Ember, on the other hand, would fight a demon with her bare hands bound behind her back before she'd retreat.

"*Move toward the law enforcer,*" Chaos said. "*I sense a rift.*"

"A rift?" I clamped my mouth shut. I seriously had to stop talking to the voice in my head.

"What?" Ember closed the door. "Did you say a rift?"

"*A tear in the fabric of the veil. A hole.*"

"Yes, I know what a rift is." I rolled my eyes.

Ember narrowed hers. "What's wrong with you? You're not making sense."

I ground my teeth. "Sorry, I misunderstood you. I think I sense a rift in the veil. Like a hole or something."

She cocked her head. "How? What does it feel like?"

"Umm... Different?"

Chaos grunted. "*The other realm has a lower vibration. I sense it bleeding through.*"

Think, Ash. What spell could I cast to sense the change in vibration? Ember knew I couldn't just *feel* something like that. An unmasking incantation like the one I used in Cinder's room wouldn't work. That would just show magic, not the difference in energies between worlds.

"Different how?" She jerked her head toward Chief Higgins to indicate I should follow.

"I don't know. It's just a feeling. Give me a second to figure it out." Dry leaves crunched beneath my shoes, and I racked my brain to think of a spell to pick up on what Chaos could naturally sense. Of course! I'd found a boundary-locating spell in one of the older tomes that could identify the perimeter of a hex keeping someone or something in one place. That could work, but I'd need to head back to the van for the potion kit.

Wariness drew Higgins' face into a scowl, making him look either nauseated or constipated. I didn't know him well enough to determine which. He had a thick black book tucked under his arm, and when we approached, he shoved it toward me. "This look familiar?"

The second my skin touched the leather cover, foreboding magic seeped into my fingers, chilling me to the marrow. I shoved it against his chest and jerked my hands back, rubbing my palms together. "Next time, warn me when you're sending dark magic my way so I can protect myself."

I focused on the tiny flame burning in my soul, imagining the light filling my body before creating a protective bubble around me. It wouldn't stop an attack if the book was hexed, but it would keep the sticky, icky magic from seeping into my skin.

I held out my hands, and he gave it back to me. "This isn't ours, if that's what you're implying."

"Where did you get it?" Ember peered over my shoulder and visibly shivered. As far as we knew, our coven had one dark magic book that our great-great-great grandmother had confiscated from a bad witch way back when. She'd locked it in a vault in the cellar, and no one had seen it since.

"Jason Monroe had it." Higgins used his tongue to move the toothpick from one side of his mouth to the other while he looked us up and down. "Said he and his friends got it from the thrift shop in town and used it for a séance but they contacted more than a ghost."

I cracked open the book and flipped through a couple of pages. Drawings of demons, dark spells, and demonic sigils filled it from margin to margin. Someone had scribbled notes in the white space as well. The librarian in me wanted to gasp and clutch my pearls, but I highly doubted a dark magic practitioner cared much for book etiquette.

"A witch could easily summon a shedim demon with that book."

Maybe so, but a human couldn't unless the rift in the veil existed before they started the incantation. "I'm going to put this in the van. We'll have to lock it in our vault."

Higgins nodded. "Whatever it takes to keep your wicked spells out of the kids' hands."

"I told you it isn't ours." I gave Higgins the stink eye before turning on my heel and marching away.

"Is there a rift here?" I whispered.

"Just past the spruce tree in the clearing. You must close it, or others may escape."

I hit the key fob to unlock the van and slid open the side door. In the bottom of the secret compartment lay another even more secret hidey-hole that only Ember and I knew about. Two taps of my index finger, my ring finger, index again, and then my pinkie unlocked the hatch. I slipped the book inside, tapped out the key backward to lock it, and grabbed the brown satchel containing our travel spell kit.

"Why do you care if others escape? You're Chaos. Wouldn't it please you to see our world fall under demon control?"

"Nothing would please me less. We must have balance. Order and chaos must be matched, or both our worlds would implode."

"Well, when you put it that way." I locked the van and jogged toward the clearing.

Ember parked her hands on her hips and squared off with the chief. "Did you call us here for help or to accuse us? You said yourself the missing kids are human."

"I said they aren't on the coven roster you gave me. They could be new recruits." He took the toothpick out of his mouth and tucked it behind his ear.

It was a good thing Ember didn't have her sword because the look on her face said she was ready to draw it and take his head clean off.

"We don't recruit." I stood next to her, resting my hand on her arm to calm her. "People are either born with magic or they aren't. If they are, they find us. I promise you, our coven had nothing to do with this, but we will find out what happened."

His gaze cut from Ember to me, his posture relaxing marginally. "Do you think it could be related to the fire in the old cemetery?"

I did my best to keep a neutral expression. "I thought they decided a discarded cigarette started it."

He shrugged. "Seems odd the ground fire had been extinguished while the trees were ablaze. I'll leave you to it." He grabbed the toothpick and put it back in his mouth.

Ew. "Heat rises." I returned his shrug and headed for the rift before he could ask any more questions.

"Can you believe that guy?" Ember fumed beside

me. "After all the help we've given him... The safety we provide to the people of Salem." Her hands curled into fists, her energy shifting, vibrating more intensely like she was about to summon her fire.

"Cool it, Em. We don't need you setting the forest alight. That's my job."

"Right here," Chaos said.

"No kidding." I stopped in my tracks. Three feet in front of me lay a summoning ring the size of my bedroom. A thick line of salt encircled the space, and half-melted black candles sat on the inside where the five points of the pentagram would have been if they'd bothered to finish the spell. "We're lucky the *kids* didn't burn down the forest. Jeez."

Ember let out a long breath. "Is this what you felt? But they couldn't have summoned anything like what the kid described unless they had help."

"You think we've got a rogue witch in town?" I set the bag at my feet and rummaged through it for my supplies. A bit of horehound, some heather, and dandelion ought to do the trick.

She shook her head. "How? We would know. We have the Witch Watcher in place. It would have sounded the bell if a new witch stayed in the city limits for more than twenty-four hours."

I crushed the herbs in a small copper bowl and poured in the lavender oil. "Have you been reinforcing it? The spell has to be invigorated every two weeks."

"Cinder always did that." Her voice sounded tiny, her gaze drifting to the grass.

"And Mom before her," I said. "It's the duty of the High Priestess."

"Well, shit." She plopped cross-legged on the ground next to me. "What about that book? Aren't you supposed to scan the resale and tourist shops to confiscate all the real magic before kids like Jason Monroe and his buddies can get their hands on them?"

I blew out a hard breath. "We've both gotten behind in our duties."

"Maybe a power grab by one of the older witches wouldn't be such a bad thing." She bumped her shoulder against mine.

"Don't say that. Leading this coven is our birthright. We can't help it if we weren't prepared for all hell to break loose. A little fire, please?" I held the bowl up, and she pointed her finger, shooting out a controlled flame as if it were the easiest thing in the world to do. For her, it probably was. I rose to my feet and brushed the leaves from my jeans.

"Don't step inside the circle."

"Thanks, genius."

Ember clambered up next to me. "What's that supposed to mean?"

Crap. Recover! "Gorgeous? It means you're beautiful, silly."

"Oh."

Holding the bowl in front of my face, I whispered the incantation and blew the smoke into the circle. It spiraled upward, coating the inner rim in a translucent haze. Near the opposite side, not quite in the center, the smoke gathered, darkening into a thick mass before disappearing through the rift. "Found it."

Ember's mouth dropped open. "How in the hell...?"

"*Back up,*" Chaos demanded. When I didn't follow his order, he boomed, nearly splitting my skull, "*He is drawn to my power. Back up now!*"

"Who?" My gaze snapped to the smoky tear in the veil, where a charcoal arm with thick talons protruding from each finger jutted through. "Oh, crap! The demon!"

I backpedaled, grabbing Ember's arm and dragging her away from the summoning ring. A muscular shoulder appeared next. Then the side of a thick neck, and finally the fiend's head. He had a wide face with a flat nose like a pug. A set of four-inch spiraling horns grew from his forehead, and as he snarled and pulled the rest of his body through the rift, black drool dribbled down his chin.

Ember yanked from my grasp and stalked toward it—typical Em—while my heart lodged in my throat and my feet froze to the ground—typical me. "Ember, you're unarmed!" I shouted, and then I whispered, "What should we do?"

"Don't move."

"I couldn't if I tried." Ice flushed my veins, and my knees wobbled. I had never come face to face with a demon before, and let me tell you, I was not reacting the way a witch should. I should have been casting spells and kicking butt. Instead, my knees nearly buckled, and every spell I'd ever memorized evaporated from my mind as if I'd set a pot of my memories to boil on the stove and forgotten about it.

The demon growled, stepping one clawed foot back and shifting his weight, preparing to lunge at my sister. Em stood literally two feet away from the monster. It would take three seconds for him to fillet her. I couldn't let that happen.

"Hey, ugly," I shouted, my feet still glued to the ground. "When was the last time you brushed your teeth?"

The demon's eyes snapped toward me, and his lips peeled back over jagged fangs, showing me no one had ever introduced him to a toothbrush.

"Careful, Ash. I cannot protect you without my corporeal form."

"Holland witches don't need protection." I don't know why Chaos's statement rubbed me the wrong way, but it did. I must've been channeling Ember's ego because I stomped forward, rubbing my palms together, ready to burn this bastard to the ground.

My fingers sparked, and I curled them toward my palms, lighting flames in both hands. Ember held a fireball the size of a cantaloupe.

"Fire won't harm a demon."

"This is magical fire." I wound up like a baseball pitcher and hurled the biggest flames I could create at the demon. They bounced off the circle and landed in the dried leaves.

The demon roared and lunged. His horns smacked the perimeter, jarring him, and he careened back, falling on his butt. Don't you know that pissed him off? He shot to his feet and rammed into the magic again. A shockwave pulsed from the circle.

"The cage holds."

"Not for long. Ember, go get your sword. We've got to banish this sucker before he breaks free." Grabbing my bag, I stomped out the flames, backed away from the circle, and dropped the kit on the ground. I wiped the copper bowl with an enchanted tissue to neutralize the magical residue and assembled the ingredients for a binding spell. I added the final component—a single drop of peppermint oil—and the concoction released a puff of purple smoke before turning to a fine powder.

I held up my hand and whispered a prayer to the goddess before casting my spell. "Standing tall or on your knees, in the name of the goddess, I force you to freeze."

I blew the powder toward the demon as Ember bounded back with her sword clasped in both hands. But the spell hit the circle's perimeter and shot back toward me. "Son of a bison!"

The enchantment wrapped around me like a magical boa constrictor, squeezing just tight enough that I couldn't move my arms and rooting my feet to the ground.

"Interesting." Ember reached for the circle, and her fingertips pressed against the invisible barrier. "Nothing can get in or out. I've never seen a ring like this cast before."

"That is because the magic used was meant to trap a demon. Only those who practice the dark arts use it."

"It's a demon cage. Of course you haven't." I struggled against the spell, which was pointless. I'd cast the strongest one I knew, and no, I could not unbind myself. What would be the point if it were that easy to escape? Another witch would have to release me, but my sister was preoccupied.

Ember pretended to lunge at the demon, laughing as she feinted right, then left. The fiend was not amused in the slightest. He roared and rammed against the magic. A sound like cracking glass reverberated through the clearing.

"Would you mind unbinding me before that creature kills us both?"

My sister winked at the demon, getting in one last taunt before she recited the unbinding incantation. Lucky for me, Ember had that one ingrained in her vim and didn't require a potion. The hold on me disintegrated, and I stumbled, dropping to my knees.

"We'll have to break the circle before we can banish him." I dumped the contents of my bag on the ground, scrambling to find the right ingredients—again—to make the potion. "I'll bind him; you stab him."

"The shedim has two hearts. Both must be pierced to vanquish him."

Well, wasn't that hunky dory? "Where? Side by side?" I whispered under my breath.

"In the center of his chest, one above the other."

I crushed the herbs with a pestle and looked at Ember. "I've been learning about demons. If this is the kind I think it is, he'll have two hearts in the center of his chest." I pointed to the two spots on my body where I imagined they would be. "You have to pierce both to vanquish him."

"I am so glad you're a bookworm." She spun her sword at her side. "I'd have just taken off his head."

I unscrewed the cap on the peppermint oil and tipped it toward the bowl. Nothing came out. "Crapity crap. I used the last drop in the spell that bounced off the circle."

"Can you improvise?" Ember's eyes grew wide, and I followed her gaze toward the circle.

The demon crouched at the far side and took off like a sprinter, ramming the perimeter and shattering the spell. He was free, and we were screwed.

CHAPTER

SIX

The shedim ran straight at me. My heart didn't just leap into my throat; it tried to escape through my nose. Ember jumped in front of the beast and swung her sword, giving me a chance to scoop up an armful of ingredients and get the hell away. I ducked behind a tree trunk and laid out what I'd nabbed, hoping to Hades I'd packed an extra bottle of peppermint oil...or at least stashed a York patty or something. Peppermint was essential for this spell to hold.

"Improvise faster!" Ember called above the racket of demon snarls and sword slashes. She grunted like she had the wind knocked out of her. Then the demon wailed. Payback was a bitch.

"Why would your sister taunt such a demon? He will shred her once he is finished playing with her."

"If you both would can it for a minute, I might be able to stop that from happening." I tossed aside a bottle of lavender oil. It might slow the beast down, but I needed something sharp and quick if I wanted to bind him. "In answer to your question, that's Ember for you. Hot-headed, quick-tempered badass, who's the most loyal witch you'll ever meet."

He scoffed. *"Witches are only loyal to themselves."*

"Says the demon who's helping me vanquish another demon." Lemon grass, chamomile, bee balm. If I wanted to give this guy the best nap of his life, I'd be set. Wait... That wasn't a bad idea. A relaxation spell combined with what I had of a binding potion could slow him down enough for Ember to do her thing.

"Does the shedim have any immunity to magic that I should know of? I mean, aside from being impervious to fire?" I uncorked the lavender and chamomile when my gaze locked on the bottle of spearmint by my right foot. This just might work.

"Sadly, none of us do, or I wouldn't be in this predicament."

"Good to hear." I put a drop of each oil into the bowl. Nothing happened. "Shitake mushrooms. Come on!" I stirred the contents and peeked from my hiding spot behind the tree.

Ember grasped her sword in both hands and swung it over her head, spinning in a circle as her right leg swept out and connected with the demon's ankle. The demon flailed backward, but he caught himself before his ass could meet dirt. My sister was so good at pissing off her foe. The shedim swiped a taloned claw forward, catching her t-shirt and tearing it nearly in two.

"That was my favorite top, you sorry sack of incubus jizz." She slashed again, ripping into his thigh. His pained screech nearly tore my head in half.

"He's angry. She will not last much longer."

"Whatever gave you that idea?" I whispered the incantations: first the binding spell in hopes that the spearmint would be strong enough, and then the relaxation invocation. The potion simmered. Then it sizzled. Then it popped, and a green flame shot out six inches from the bowl. "Huh. That's new."

"Have you tried this spell before?" I didn't appreciate the wariness in his voice.

"Apparently, this is my day to step out of my comfort zone." The potion turned to black granules, like fresh ground pepper, rather than the powder I expected.

"Will it work?"

"Only one way to find out." I poured the grains into my palm and fisted my hand. Pushing to my feet, I peered around the tree to gauge the demon's location. At least one of the Holland sisters had to look before she leaped.

Ember stabbed the fiend in the gut. It wailed and jerked away, wrenching the sword from her grasp. Black goo oozed from the wound as it yanked the sword from its belly and tossed it aside.

"Any day now, Ash." Ember grabbed a set of daggers from her ankle holster.

With the demon's back toward me, I whispered a silencing spell so I could attack in stealth mode. My feet pounded the ground, but I made no sound as I darted toward it.

Ember jabbed her dagger into its shoulder. It swung its arm, claws raking my sister's stomach. A pained shout ripped from her throat, and she doubled over.

I hurled the enchanted granules at the beast's backside. They stuck to him like ticks on a dog before absorbing into his ashy skin. He lifted his arm again, his movements slow and heavy.

"That's the best I could do. Are you okay?" I grabbed Ember's sword and ran toward her, ready to stab the fiend through both his hearts. She couldn't hear me, thanks to my silencing spell.

"Oh no." Ember made a grabby motion with her hands. "This is personal. He's mine."

Who was I to steal her chance at retribution? I handed her the sword.

"Never mess with a Holland witch." She jabbed the sword into the center of his chest and twisted. The razor edge sliced up and then down, creating a foot-long gash.

The demon stumbled back and let out a skull-splitting screech that would have the whole town wondering what kind of animal died in the woods. I guess I should've cast the silencing spell on all of us.

Ember doubled over again, her sword and daggers toppling to the ground. I clutched her shoulders, bracing her as the demon wailed again before crumbling to bits and being sucked back into the rift.

"Show me where he got you." I tried to lower her to the ground, but she shrugged me off. "Ember..."

Oh, right. The silencing spell. "What I've done is now undone. As I will it, so mote it be."

"The shedim's claws are tipped with poison. If he broke skin, she will need a healer to draw out the toxins."

"Show me." I peeled her hands away from the wound. Three bloody slashes stretched diagonally from her rib cage to her hip. "We need to get you to Patrice. You need a healer."

She spoke through gritted teeth. "You have to close the rift. More demons can come through, and there's no circle to contain them."

The adrenaline in my veins chose this moment to dissipate, allowing a wave of fatigue to wash over me. I must've cast at least six spells in the last twenty minutes. My vim was waning hardcore, taking my thoughts with it.

"How? What spell will seal it?" I asked.

She laughed and then winced. "You're the smart one. I thought you had the entire library memorized."

If only. "A patch, maybe? A little help, please?" My question was intended for Chaos since he seemed to be an expert in the matter.

Ember replied, "Yeah. We'll need to get closer." She reached for me, and I helped her walk to the rift.

"The fibers of the veil are thin like strands of silk. They'll need to be woven back together for a permanent hold."

Weaving the fabric of reality. With this level of fatigue and Ember's injuries? Yeah, right. "We'd need a few more witches to have the power to seal it for good. I can make a glue, though. It'll hold long enough for us to call in reinforcements."

"Yeah. Do that." Ember leaned forward, bracing her hands on her knees. "Fast."

I grabbed my bag and dumped the contents back inside before racing around the tree where I'd left the rest of the supplies and stuffing those in too.

Back at the rift, Ember's complexion had taken on a grayish hue. We didn't have much time. My hands trembled as I mixed the ingredients for the magical glue. Angelica, basil, and heather turned to green liquid when I poured in the wormwood oil.

"The poison will solidify her innards before turning her skin to ash."

"I'm working as fast as I can." The potion popped and sizzled. I grabbed Ember's hand to channel her magic, which I felt really, *really* bad about. She needed all her strength to fight the poison, but I couldn't do this alone.

"A simple patch to close this hatch. As I say, keep the demons at bay." I tossed the potion at the hole in the veil, and the torn sides moved toward each other, sticking together. A thick scar ran down the length of it, but as soon as the perimeter spell wore off, no one would be able to see it.

Ember sagged, my stubborn sister refusing to give in. After grabbing my bag and her weapons, I wrapped her arm over my shoulders, and we stumbled to the van together. I buckled her into the passenger seat and tossed our gear into the back before texting Patrice to let her know we needed her.

The drive took ten excruciating minutes. I fought to keep my eyes open and on the road while Ember rested her head against the window, her eyes closed, mouth open. Ghostly white rimmed her lips, and her shallow breathing seemed forced.

"We've got time, right? She can come back from this?" I didn't bother whispering. Even if Ember were awake, I doubted she'd remember me talking to "myself."

Chaos grunted. *"I've never seen someone survive a*

shedim attack. You are strong witches, but the poison is spreading quickly."

"Fabulous." I came to a screeching halt in front of Patrice's house and laid on the horn.

She scurried out, wearing a long, flowy brown skirt and a light pink top. She'd piled her curly red hair on top of her hair in a messy bun, and a pair of reading glasses hung from a chain around her neck.

I slammed the door and ran around to Ember's side before pulling her out. Her eyes rolled back and her head lolled to the left as we dragged her inside and laid her on an exam table.

"What happened?" Patrice cut Ember's shirt the rest of the way open. The skin around the wounds looked like partially burnt charcoal...just like the demon's.

"It's demon poison. A shedim got in one good swipe before she vanquished him. Can you draw it out?"

"I'll do my best." She dumped jars of herbs and liquids into a bowl. Normally, I'd watch her intently, trying to learn as much as I could about her spells, but this time, I kept my gaze trained on my sister's paling face.

"Patrice will fix you, Em." I gripped her hand in mine. Her finger twitched, but she didn't have the strength to hold me. "I'm so sorry I didn't get the demon under control faster."

"Not...your fault," she whispered.

"Yes, it is. I take full responsibility. I should have checked the perimeter to see if the binding spell would penetrate it before I wasted the powder." And if I'd kept the kit stocked properly, I would've had enough peppermint oil to make a second proper binding spell.

"You are not to blame. If she hadn't taunted the beast, he would not have been so strong. His anger increased his power."

"If I'd kept up with the thrift shops, I could have nabbed that book before it got into the wrong hands. I can list a million reasons why this is my fault." A sob bubbled from my chest to my throat. "I can't lose you too, Em. You have to be okay."

Ember groaned, and I snapped my gaze to Patrice. She chanted the incantation and returned to my sister's side.

"The blame lies with those who summoned the shedim."

"Shut up." I could appreciate what Chaos was trying to do, but damn. If I wanted to wallow in self-pity, he needed to let me.

"I didn't say anything." Patrice narrowed her eyes at me.

"Sorry. Talking to the voice in my head. It's been a day." I laughed dryly.

"So it seems." She spooned the mixture over

Ember's wounds, and it disappeared beneath her skin.

Em gasped, her bloodshot eyes flying open as she clawed at the table. She thrashed, and a gurgling sound emanated from her throat.

"What's happening? This isn't helping; it's hurting her!" I tightened my grip on her hand, trying to hold her steady.

Patrice grabbed her other arm. "The potion is traveling through her body, collecting the poison."

Ember's legs flailed. Her knee drew upward and crashed into my shoulder before her boot thudded on the table. Ouch. That would leave a bruise, for sure. She went utterly still. Her chest didn't rise and fall with her breath. Her hand fell limp in mine.

"Is she…?" My voice trembled.

"Wait for it…" Patrice snatched an oversized Mason jar from a shelf and twisted off the lid.

Ember's wounds bubbled. Black sludge pooled in the gashes.

"Take this." Patrice shoved a ginormous syringe into my hand. "Draw out the poison and put it in the jar."

I did as I was told, sticking the tip of the device into my sister's stomach and pulling on the plunger. Thick liquid slowly filled the vial, and I squirted it into the jar. When I returned to the wound, it had already refilled with more sludge. I sucked out the poison again while Patrice worked on the other side.

We filled six vials a piece, the liquid reaching the jar's rim before Ember's own flesh and blood were visible in the gashes. Patrice hovered her hands above the wounds and whispered another incantation.

Ember gasped, her hands flying to her face as she looked around wildly. "What...?"

"Shh...shh..." I took her hand again, and this time, she held me back. "The demon poisoned you, but we get it all out. You're going to be okay." I looked at Patrice for confirmation, and she nodded.

"These gashes require sutures. Give me a minute to gather my supplies." She patted Ember on the leg before turning and leaving the room. Patrice wasn't just a witchy healer. She was also a nurse practitioner. Lucky us.

"Your healer is talented."

"We've got the best of the best in our coven."

Ember lifted herself onto her elbows. "We sure do. What kind of spell did you throw on him? He looked like he was moving through molasses."

I shrugged. "I had to combine two spells since I didn't have enough oil for another binding."

"Well, it worked." She winced and laid her head down. "Good job."

I scoffed. "Hardly."

"You don't take compliments well."

Not when I didn't deserve them.

"Here we are. This will sting a little." Patrice held

up a syringe of what I assumed to be numbing medicine.

Ember laughed. "I've been through worse."

"What happened out there, anyway? How did a shedim get through the veil?" She injected the wounds and threaded a hooked needle.

"Apparently, some wannabe witches got ahold of an actual dark magic grimoire." I shook my head. "They never should have gotten their hands on it."

Patrice pursed her lips as she sewed. "A mundane wouldn't be able to summon a demon. Someone had to have witch ancestry, at least."

"They could if the veil was already open," Ember said. "We found a rift in the center of their summoning circle."

"How did it get there?" she asked.

"Good question." My brow furrowed. "And how would they know where to find it in the first place? We had to cast a spell to locate it."

"Maybe the demon drew them there," Ember said. "A beast that powerful can't slip through the veil, even with how thin it is here. Ghouls and fae, sure. That's what our job is for, but something with that much magical power would need to be summoned."

The veil was good about that...keeping the baddest of the bad on the side where they belonged. The more magic an entity possessed, the harder it was to cross into our world.

"That is precisely what happened. The shedim sensed the people in the forest and drew them to the rift. Once they performed the summoning, he was free to pass through in both directions."

"That's got to be it," I said. I bet they really did want to have a fun little séance. Poor kids. I couldn't imagine what the demon did to them after he pulled them through the rift. If they were lucky, moving from our world to the other killed them instantly. The mundane couldn't exist in their physical form in the spirit realm.

"What about the circle?" Ember asked. "Someone had to be a witch to put it up."

"We'll have to talk to Jason and see what he knows about his friends. I bet Patrice is right about the ancestry. If not for that circle, the shedim would be running rampant in Salem."

Patrice tied the last stitch and cut the thread. "But that leads us back to the question of how the rift got there in the first place. If it wasn't just a thin spot, someone created it. Purposely or not. Could there be an uprising on the other side?"

"There is no uprising." A low growl rumbled between my ears. *"Summoning a Prince of Hell can fracture the veil. The threads weaken and tear. It has happened before."*

Fantastic. It was my fault after all.

SEVEN

"How are you still awake? I feel like I'm about to keel over, and all I did was cast a few spells." I unlocked the back door and held it open for Ember.

She trudged through and grabbed the handrail to haul herself up the stairs. "Casting spells can be more taxing than fighting, and you performed what? Five? How are *you* still awake?"

Eight if you counted the location and exorcism spells I tried before she got to the shop, but she didn't need to know about those. I helped her onto the couch and took off her boots before turning on the television. A reporter with a solemn expression told the story of the kids. The police would be holding a press conference in an hour.

Ember's phone chimed, and she groaned, wincing

as she dug it out of her pocket. "It's the chief wanting an update. I better call him."

"'Kay. I'll make dinner." I kicked off my Mary Janes and padded to the kitchen while she dialed the chief.

"Your body requires rest."

"No shit, Captain Obvious. It also requires food." I rummaged through the fridge and found a bag of fresh mushrooms, some spinach, and half a rotisserie chicken. The pantry offered dried pasta and a jar of spaghetti sauce. A trip to the grocery store was in order, but I had enough for tonight.

"Chicken spaghetti it is." I poured some olive oil into a pan and dumped in the spinach and mushrooms to sauté them. "Now that I've got you alone, I need answers." The mushrooms sizzled in the oil, the spinach wilting as I pushed it around the pan. "Since I caused this trouble, how do I fix it? Will sending you back heal the veil?"

He didn't answer.

I set a big pot of water to boil and opened the jar of sauce. "Hello, Chaos? Are you still there?"

He waited a full thirty seconds before he said, *"I was not the first Prince to be released."*

"Whoa. Wait… What?" Spaghetti sauce splashed onto the stove as I dumped it in the pot. I didn't bother to clean it up. Yeah, it would be stuck on good from the heat of cooking, but…

"You're telling me someone else summoned one of your brothers?"

"Discord either escaped or was released a time ago. I haven't sensed him in this realm, but my power is limited while in your human form."

"Can you elaborate on 'a time ago,' please? How long ago?" I swirled a wooden spoon in the sauce.

"Time runs differently across the veil. I don't know."

"And why would someone want to summon one of you?"

"To harness our power."

"But you're Princes of Hell. Couldn't you just swipe your claws and poison them? You said yourself you've never seen anyone survive a fight with the shedim, and he was a mid-level demon. Surely no one could contain you."

His growl tickled my chest. I hated to admit it, but I kinda like it when he did that. *"Only a witch with immense power could contain a Prince. Like you, for example."*

I laughed. "Only a screwup like me could *accidentally* contain you."

"You have no concept of your power."

"Anyway..." My cheeks heated. We'd already established I didn't take compliments well, so why did he keep dishing them out? And why was I blushing over a *demon's* opinion of me? *Get it together, Ash.*

"We are also known to make deals. Demons of any level will do a witch's bidding for a price."

"Let me guess. The price is usually their soul." I dumped the pasta into the boiling water.

"Precisely."

"So, it's possible there's a rogue witch in Salem who summoned Discord, a Prince of Hell, to do their bidding, and they sold their soul to do whatever it is they want to do. And said witch also cast the summoning circle the kids used in the forest this morning."

"The witch would not have to be rogue. Desperation makes people act out of character. Demons prey on that weakness."

"Well, crappity crap." It could be a coven member, or it could not. I chopped the chicken and added it into the sauce along with the mushrooms and spinach. "On the bright side, at least I'm not the cause of it this time."

"Summoning me weakened the veil even more. I doubt that was the only rift that will need to be sealed."

"But you said no one could summon you without your skull. Is that not the case for your brothers? I'm the only thing remotely close to an Ink Master for hundreds of miles."

"You are an Ink Master, but yes, it is the case. If Discord was summoned, the witch used his skull. He will be

searching for Mayhem and me so that we may collect our price from the witch who trapped us."

"Uh-huh. And what happens if he finds you... trapped inside me?"

"He will kill you."

"Holy frak." The timer buzzed, so I drained the water and dished up the food. "And what happens if I can't find your skull? Will you be a voice inside my head forever? I mean, if your brother doesn't find us?"

He went silent again, and that made an emptiness form in the pit of my stomach. "Let me guess. I'm not going to like your answer."

"How did you know?"

"You got quiet. That's your tell. When it's bad news, you'd rather say nothing."

"A demon cannot coexist with his host indefinitely."

I waited for him to elaborate, but he didn't. My insides twisted into a knot, the food suddenly not smelling nearly as enticing as it had a moment ago. "Chaos, what will happen to me?"

"I will take over, and you will simply be a voice in my head. Then you will cease to exist."

The knot in my stomach rose to my throat. I swallowed hard. "How?"

"My soul will bind with your body. Your current form will erode, and mine will be born from it."

That sounded like a goddess-damned horror movie. I imagined my flesh falling off in chunks as a monstrous face ripped from my abdomen, tearing me in half. A shiver ran up my spine.

"Why would you do that?" My voice was barely a whisper.

"I would have no choice in the matter. The process has already begun. Hence, the importance of finding my skull."

Hellhounds and hand grenades. What the actual eff had I done? This couldn't be happening. I was... And he... And the rifts... My hands trembled, so I set the plates on the counter. "What are we going to do?"

"What's taking so long?" Ember shouted from the living room. "I'm so hungry I could eat a donkey's ass."

"First, you will take care of your physical bodies. You'll be useless otherwise. Then you will locate my skull and return me to my corporeal form. Once I am free, you will find the witch who summoned Discord and put an end to her madness. Only then will your city find peace."

"Ash?" Ember called.

"Coming..." I picked up the plates and slowly made my way to the living room.

Caring for our physical bodies, I could handle. Finding Chaos's skull might be an issue, but I could go it alone. Freeing him should be as easy as trapping him was. Battling a witch who had a Prince of Hell in her pocket...that was Ember's department.

Well, shit. "I can't do all this alone."

"You must tell Ember what you've done. Her skills may

be required to retrieve my skull. I doubt it was left unguarded.”

“But you’re a demon,” I whispered right before I entered the room.

“She is your sister. She will understand your mishap.”

Would she? I wasn’t so sure. “Here’s dinner.” I set our plates on the coffee table and darted back into the kitchen to grab two bottles of beer. After today, we needed something stronger, but beer would have to do.

Ember twisted off the cap and downed half the contents. “Thanks. The Chief was none too pleased when I told him what happened.”

“I bet.” I shoved a forkful of spaghetti into my mouth. “He still blames us?”

“I think I’ve convinced him we aren’t involved, but he’s suspicious. He agreed to let us talk to Jason tomorrow, though, so that’s a plus. Hopefully he can give us enough info to piece all this together.”

“What about the rift? The patch I put on it won’t hold forever.”

She finished chewing before she answered, “I already sent Shade and Chrys to take care of it.”

Great. Yet another excuse for him to gloat over me. He had the energy to repair the rift correctly when I didn’t. Forget the fact I’d done a huge amount of spell casting and helped battle a demon. That wouldn’t matter to Shade. Him fixing something I couldn't do properly would be all he needed.

My thoughts must've been clear on my face because Ember patted my knee. "Since it's been on the news, curious humans will be swarming the place. They'll need to hide what they're doing, and Shade is the best at shadow magic."

"I know that." I shoved another forkful into my mouth, but I wasn't hungry. Chaos was right. I needed to tell Ember what I'd done. I had pertinent information that she, as acting High Priestess, needed to know.

Telling her the truth was the right thing to do, but that didn't mean it would be easy. My screwup had almost gotten her killed today, and now I was about to inform her that her baby sister had a demon inside her who would take over completely if she didn't vanquish him ASAP.

"What a day, huh?" Ember took a swig from her beer. "I'm sure glad it's over."

My mouth went dry, and I felt like I'd swallowed a wad of cotton. "It's not quite done yet. I need to talk to you about something."

She spoke around a mouthful of food. "If it has to do with the library or the shop, it can wait. I'm beat."

"It doesn't. I..." Deep breath in. Let it out slowly. *You can do this, Ash.* "I accidentally summoned a demon. Not the shedim. A different one." I clamped my mouth shut, my shoulders drawing toward my ears.

Ember laughed. "Tell me, dear sister. How did you *accidentally* summon a demon?"

She didn't believe me. If Chaos hadn't been talking to me all day...helping me solve this mystery...I wouldn't believe it myself. I made mistakes all the time, but not like this.

"Show her my mark."

"You're right. I'll start with the worst and move backward from there."

Ember's brow furrowed. "What?"

I shoved my sleeve up to my elbow and held out my arm. Chaos's sigil glowed deep red. "I found this page of sigils in Cinder's room. This one is for power over chaos...or so I thought."

I ran my finger over the mark, and Chaos's growl vibrated in my chest. If I didn't know any better, I'd have said he was purring. That sounded way too content to be a growl.

"It's beautiful. You definitely got all the artistic talent in the family." She ate another bite.

"Yeah, well, it turns out this sigil belongs to a demon called Chaos."

"A Prince of—"

"A Prince of Hell to be precise. He's one of the highest-ranking demons in the realm, and I somehow called him over and trapped him inside my head."

She laughed again. "You're joking."

"I wish I were."

"You…" She took a giant bite of food, her right cheek protruding as she chewed.

I turned toward her, folding one leg beneath me. "I know it sounds nuts, but it's true. He's been talking to me all day. How do you think I knew so much about the shedim?"

"You read tons of books. You know just about everything."

"Chaos told me what we had to do. Pierce the two hearts. He also told me about the poison claws, so I knew to get you to Patrice to draw out the toxin."

She set her plate on the coffee table and chugged the rest of her beer. "If there were a demon inside you, you'd have vanquished him by now."

"I tried, believe me. The only way I can get him out of *my* head is to find *his*. A witch vanquished him way back when, but she kept his skull so he would be imprisoned in darkness across the veil. I have to find his skull in order to set him free."

That was enough for her to swallow right now. I'd save the part about him taking me over for another time.

She eyed me skeptically. "You're not playing some kind of prank, are you? Because I am in no mood for…"

I drew an X over my chest. "Cross my heart. I'm as serious as can be."

She stared at me, waiting for me to crack a smile. When I didn't, she widened her eyes. "Holy shit, Ash. A demon?"

"I know. On the plus side, he's given me some insight into the rift ordeal. Though that's not good news either."

She squeezed her eyes shut and shook her head, no doubt biting back all the profanities she wanted to sling at me. Holland witches never dabbled in dark magic. Not even by accident.

I set my mostly full plate next to hers. "Do you need time to process, or should I continue?"

She made a circle motion with her hand. "Keep going. Get it all out now before I lose my ever-loving..." She drew in a deep breath.

I cleared my throat. "The veil has been weakened, and there will be more rifts. The fibers are deteriorating because someone summoned a demon prince. Or so Chaos thinks, right?"

"*Correct.*"

I nodded. "He says yes."

She looked sideways at me. "Is that what he says? And I suppose *he* is the demon prince whose summoning caused this mess?"

I shook my head adamantly and held up my hands. "For once, this is not my fault. His brother Discord, who was also in the dark prison, got out a while ago. Chaos thinks that must be what weakened the veil. My summoning him made things worse, but I was not the catalyst."

She raked her fingers through her hair. "So someone else summoned a demon prince...Discord?"

"Right."

"Who? Why?"

I explained the conversation I'd had with Chaos in the kitchen and how it could be a rogue witch or someone from the coven. "Maybe John will reveal the culprit when we talk to him tomorrow."

She picked up her empty beer, shook it, and set the bottle back on the table. "What on earth would someone in our coven want with Discord? I can't wrap my mind around it."

I sighed. "I don't know. We don't even know how long ago he was summoned. Time is different across the veil, but..."

Ember arched a brow, silently urging me to continue, but I pulled a Chaos and kept my mouth shut. I had an idea of who...and why...and it wasn't good news.

"Talk to me, Ash. What are you thinking?"

"Activity has picked up tremendously over the past month, right? You've had more beasties to hunt than ever."

"Yeah. We're getting close to Halloween, though. The veil is at its thinnest in October."

That was true, but this seemed like too much of a

coincidence. "Wouldn't you say the activity started picking up right after Cinder disappeared?"

She froze, her mouth half open, whatever words she'd planned not making it across her lips.

I tapped the tattoo on my arm. "I found the page of sigils in Cinder's room, under a powerful spell. She was hiding them from me. From us."

"No way. Cinder would never summon a demon. She was High Priestess. She had all the power she needed. She…"

"She was desperate to find Mom and Dad. She insisted they were alive out there somewhere."

Ember kept shaking her head. "She wouldn't, Ash. A Holland witch would never summon a demon. Never."

"I did."

"By mistake. Cinder doesn't make mistakes."

"She ran off to find our parents. Her protection sigil didn't work. What if she found out what happened to Mom and Dad and summoned Discord to make a deal to find them? What if he killed her? What if she sold her soul to him to protect us? What if…?"

My mind reeled. There were too many what-ifs to consider. "Would he kill her, Chaos? If she released him from his prison, wouldn't he owe her? Or would he need to feed and kill the first person he saw?"

"Demons do not feed like ghouls," his voice rumbled

in my head. *"He would be in debt to whomever freed him."*

I blew out a breath. "Oh, good."

"However..." Silence stretched inside my head. Crap. Whatever he said next would be bad news. Again. *"If their request was not in proportion to their favor, he would require a price be paid for his assistance."*

"Oh, shit."

"What's he saying?" Ember asked.

"That any what-if scenario could be what happened."

She drummed her fingers on her knee. "We don't know Cinder is the one who started this."

"I found the page of sigils in her room. The evidence is pretty damning."

Her head still shook. "Where did you find it? I searched it and found nothing."

"You didn't look under her mattress."

"I... Wait." She pursed her lips. "Are you okay? This demon you're hosting sounds like he's been a helpful guy so far, but... You're not going to lose control and try to kill me in my sleep? He's not going to kill you?"

"I have no reason to kill your sister. I require your assistance to locate my skull, so I promise I will not take over until I have no choice."

"That's reassuring."

"It's the best I can do."

"I'm fine."

"Good." The look on Ember's face said she was shutting this conversation down. She idolized Cinder and didn't want to hear anything about our beloved big sis dipping her toes into the dark arts.

I stood and picked up the plates. "Chaos promises to be a good boy if you'll help me find his skull."

She grabbed the empty bottles and followed me to the kitchen. "First thing in the morning. If we don't recharge, we'll be useless."

"I know." I rinsed the dishes and added them to the dishwasher before scrubbing the spilled sauce from the stove.

"Seriously, Ash. The mess will be here tomorrow." She dropped the bottles into the recycle bin. "You can clean it then."

"I'm almost done."

"Your sister is right. Your body requires rest."

I rubbed a disinfecting wipe over the counter and tossed it in the trash. "Okay. Let's get some sleep. Demon's orders."

CHAPTER

EIGHT

Steam rose from the water's surface, and the scent of lavender oil wafted to my nose as I poured Epsom salt into my favorite potion. A hot bath would do wonders for my aching muscles. I slipped into the tub and sighed as the warmth engulfed me.

The sigil on my arm turned a deeper shade of crimson, and it pulsed as I ran my finger over it. Chaos rumbled inside me, the contented sensation rolling from my chest downward to my toes.

"Why do you react like that?" I traced the design.

"That mark is the closest thing to a corporeal form I have...and I haven't been touched since I was imprisoned."

"Oh." I jerked my hand away. *Good going, Ash. You were petting a demon.* I didn't want to ask exactly which part of him I was stroking.

I sucked in a breath and slid under the water, holding it as long as I could before I was forced to come up for air. Rule number one of possession: Don't get intimate with your demon.

That probably wasn't a rule, but it should have been. I had a lot of research to do.

"Do you have any tips for finding your skull? Tell me about the witch who cursed you. How did it happen?"

Silence answered, and I imagined him glowering, which was no easy feat since I didn't have a clue what he looked like. "Are you as nasty looking as the shedim? Do you have horns?"

"The witch who cursed me was immensely powerful. Her magic was stronger than any I'd seen."

"Was she your lover?" I clamped my mouth shut. Why the hell would I ask him that? I was exhausted. Borderline delirious. I needed to wash and haul my ass to bed before I talked myself into a pickle.

Thankfully, he ignored my last question. *"Your missing sister might not be the one who summoned Discord, but I believe she knows who did."*

"She must, right? Why else would she have your sigils?"

"Exactly. In my demonic form, I do have horns. I also have a human form, and I believe the saying 'beauty is in the eye of the beholder' applies. What is nasty to you could be beautiful across the veil."

"Is the shedim beautiful?"

He chuckled. *"No, he is considered one of the vilest in appearance."*

"Good to know. You don't have to answer that other question I threw out there. It's none of my business."

"I didn't plan to, and you are correct."

"Right. Good." I finished washing and pulled the plug before grabbing a fluffy blue towel and drying off. Standing in front of the mirror, I squeezed the water from my hair and wrapped the towel turban-style around my head.

"Why is your hair blue?"

I shrugged. "Why not? I like to play around with colors. It was hot pink a few months ago."

"It is a nice shade."

"Thanks." I dipped my fingers into the jar of moisturizer and spread the cool cream across my face. "I'm glad you approve."

"You're beautiful." His voice grew deeper and even more rumbly. *"Your body is exquisite."*

A warm shiver ran up my spine, a pleasant sensation right before my stomach dropped so hard it nearly splattered on the bathroom floor. "Wait. What? You can see me?"

"Mm. The view is spectacular."

I yanked the towel from my head and covered my

lady bits. "You can see through my eyes?" I nearly shrieked.

"Of course. And feel with your skin. We are bound."

"Holy Hecate." I shut off the light and darted into my room. I grabbed some underwear from my unmentionables drawer and squeezed my eyes shut before putting them on, which was no easy feat. My right leg went through the hole just fine, but my left big toe got hung up on the crotch and I did this little jumping dance across the room before falling backward onto my bed.

"Close your eyes so I can get dressed!" I unhooked my toe and shoved my leg through.

His deep chuckle rumbled all the way down to my stomach. *"I don't have eyes of my own."*

"Ugh!" I grabbed a shirt from my closet, tossed the towel into the bathroom, and spun around. Facing my full-length mirror. "Crap!"

I turned back around and pulled on the shirt. "You could have told me you see what I see."

"I assumed it was obvious."

My jaw clenched. It was obvious now that I thought about it. He'd seen the summoning circle and the demon inside it. He'd also seen me completely naked. So much for not getting intimate with my demon.

"Listen here, mister. We need some ground rules.

No more peeking when I'm not wearing clothes, and no comments about my body. Got it?"

"If I refuse to comply?"

"Then I'll sage the shit out of every room in the house. I'll make sage perfume and cook with so much sage, you'll choke." Yet another reason I should have realized he had access to my senses. He'd commented on how bad the sage smelled when I'd tried to evict him. *Use your brain, Ash.*

"I can tolerate the foul odor."

I looked in the mirror, slamming my brows over my eyes for emphasis. "For someone who claims to hate witches, you seem awfully hot and bothered."

"What can I say? It's been ages since I've seen a woman as beautiful as you."

"Since you've seen *any* woman." I turned off the lights and climbed into bed, sliding my feet beneath the sheets. "I'm done. No talking while I'm trying to sleep."

"Your body is stressed. You should pleasure yourself to relieve the tension."

"You'd like that, wouldn't you? Perve."

"What man wouldn't? Give it a try." He made that purring noise again that filled my whole body with warm fuzzies.

"Stop that. I mean it. I'm going to sleep, and when I wake up, I expect an apology for these unwanted advances." Leave it to me to possess myself with not only a Prince of Hell, but a horny one at that.

He chuckled. *"Understood."*

I lay back and was out the moment my head hit the pillow.

Firm hands slid down my sides before agile fingers toyed with the band of my panties. Lips grazed my stomach, and I reached out to grasp muscular shoulders. His breath, hot against my skin, raised goosebumps on my flesh. I gazed down, and he looked at me with eyes as green as emeralds. He grinned wickedly, and the black of his pupils bled outward, filling his irises before consuming the whites. My pulse thrummed, though not from fear. He pressed his lips to my naval before gliding his tongue downward and sliding my underwear from my hips. Gripping my thighs, he blew a warm breath across my center, and my entire body tingled with need.

"Ash!" My sister's voice cut through the room, and I bolted upright, awakened from my dream. "Why are you still in bed? We have to talk to Jason in half an hour. Let's go." She turned on her heel and left my bedroom door open as she marched down the hall.

My pulse still sprinting, I swallowed the dryness

from my mouth and threw off the covers. "What the hell, Chaos?"

"*I'm sorry.*"

"You better be. How dare you put those images into my mind? I wanted to sleep, not have sexy dreams about the demon in my head."

"*You...*" Surprise laced his voice, and I imagined a quizzical expression in those emerald eyes of his.

"You really are a perve, you know that?" I stomped to the bathroom to brush my teeth.

"*I'm sorry about the things I said last night. As I mentioned, I have been imprisoned for ages. I should not have spoken like that to you, but I didn't put images into your head. Whatever dreams you had, sexy or not, they were your own.*"

I spit and rinsed. "Yeah, right."

"*I promise I didn't violate you in your sleep, but I notice you woke up quite aroused.*" A smile played in his voice. I could practically see the amusement in his eyes.

"It was just a dream," I grumbled as I brushed my hair. "You didn't experience it too, did you? Where do you go when I sleep?"

"*My consciousness goes dormant too, and I had my own dreams, which weren't nearly as pleasurable as yours.*"

Fantastic. He came on to me, yet *I* had the inappropriate dreams. Figured.

I got dressed, doing my best to avoid looking in the mirror or at any part of my body. After getting ready for the day, I found Ember standing in the kitchen, her arms crossed.

"Finally." She tossed me a granola bar and motioned to the tumbler of coffee on the counter. "We're late."

"He's being held for psychiatric evaluation. It's not like he's going anywhere." I shoved half the bar into my mouth and carried the coffee downstairs. It was hot as hellfire, but I sucked down as much as I could on the drive to the hospital and popped a mint into my mouth before we headed inside.

Frigid air blasted my skin as the doors slid open, and the sterile scents of bleach and antiseptic made my nose tingle. We hung a left and paced down the hall toward the psychiatric ward. Fluorescent lights hummed from above, tinting the white walls and floor in a greenish-yellow hue.

"What is this place?" Chaos asked.

"It's a hospital. I guess a demon wouldn't have much need for medical professionals."

"It's not like any hospital I've seen."

"It's exactly like every hospital I've seen." I jogged to catch up with Ember.

"You look like you belong in this ward when you talk to him like that. Put in an ear bud so you can pretend to be on the phone." She stopped outside a door. "What's he saying?"

"He's never seen a hospital like this."

"What did they look like in his time?" she asked.

"Dark. Rancid stench. The candles had exposed flames rather than being held behind glass in the ceiling."

"Whoa." I tugged my ear buds from my pocket and put one in my ear. "He's from before hospitals had electric lights."

"I hate to break it to you, buddy." Ember knocked on the door and peered through the little square window. "If your skull was stolen before Salem had electricity, it might not exist anymore. We're looking at your vanquishing happening at least one hundred fifty years ago. Maybe longer."

"It must exist. Discord was freed."

"So were you, kinda," I said. "You're trapped in me now, but you're not in prison. Maybe another Ink Master made the same mistake as me."

"Let's hope not. Otherwise, your life will end soon."

I flinched at his words. "Thanks for the reminder."

"What did he say?" Ember asked.

Chief Higgins opened the door, and thankfully, I didn't have to answer. My sister had enough on her plate right now without worrying about my impending doom.

"His story hasn't changed since yesterday," Higgins said as he stepped into the hall. "He's sedated, so I don't know how much help he's going to be."

"Any details he can provide will help us get to the bottom of it." Ember caught the door before it could close and stepped inside. I followed without making eye contact. I was still miffed at the chief for blaming us.

Jason Monroe lay in the bed by the window. The curtains were open, and he squinted against the sunlight. Ember walked around the bed and pulled them halfway closed.

"Better?" she asked.

He nodded and stared blankly ahead.

"I'm Ember, and this is my sister, Ash. We'd like you to tell us about what happened yesterday. Can you do that?"

"I already told Higgins and three of his officers. I'm not talking to any more police." He slurred his words, an effect of the drugs they pumped into him.

I stood at the foot of the bed and rested my fingers on the plastic. Jason's hair was a mess, his eyes rimmed with red. Otherwise, he looked completely unscathed. "We aren't police."

"What then? Reporters?" He crossed his arms. "I'm not crazy."

"We know," Ember said.

"How did you escape the monster?" I asked, and his gaze flicked to mine. "You said it pulled your friends through an invisible hole. How did you get away?"

"I shouldn't have." He clasped his hands in his lap and lowered his eyes.

"But you did." Ember touched her fingertips to his shoulder. "And we need to know how."

He laughed dryly. "I wasn't inside the circle."

"And the other kids were?" Why on earth would they be inside a summoning circle?

"Amanda said it would protect us. That we should stay inside it while we held the séance, and no spirits could harm us. She, Andrew, and Caitlyn did what she told them. I was showing off, trying to impress Caitlyn by being the tough guy. But the circle didn't protect them. It trapped them." He choked on a sob.

My heart ached for the poor guy. This Amanda chick either didn't know what she was doing, or she meant to sacrifice her friends. Or both. "I know it's hard to relive this, but tell us about Amanda. Is she the one who brought the book? Did she claim to be a witch?"

He toyed with the edge of the blanket and shook his head. "The book was Caitlyn's. She collects old stuff, found it at a thrift store forever ago. She's used it before and nothing happened, so I don't know how..." A tear slid down his cheek. He didn't bother to wipe it away.

"And Amanda?" Ember asked.

"Andrew met her last week. We were hanging out in Caitlyn's basement, drinking, when Amanda told us she was descended from witches. She'd turned eighteen and found out the names of her birth parents. She traced her ancestry to Salem, so she came here to find her roots."

A witch who grew up human. That explained why she might not know the difference between a summoning ring and a protection circle. "Why that particular spot in the woods? Why not do it in the basement?"

He shrugged. "Amanda said witches worked in nature. The rest of us went along with it."

Ember fisted her hands, impatience carving lines in her forehead. "Why that spot? Who chose it?"

"We all did, I guess."

"Why?" I asked.

His shoulders drew toward his ears and stayed there. "You'll think I'm crazy if I tell you."

"We don't so far." Ember's teeth didn't part as she spoke, and I couldn't blame her. Getting information out of this guy was like squeezing wine from a raisin.

"We won't think you're crazy. We're trying to help figure this out." I walked around to the side of the bed, ready to strangle it out of him if he didn't hurry up.

Okay, no, I would never actually strangle someone. But Ember might.

"It felt different there. We walked into the woods

and headed straight for that spot like it *wanted* us to do the séance there."

"That makes sense." I looked at Ember, who nodded.

"It's as we suspected."

"You believe me?" Jason clutched my wrist, startling me. "Tell me you believe me."

My gaze flicked to his hand, and Chaos growled in my head. *"He shouldn't be touching you."*

Jason's eyes widened in a look of sheer terror. His grip tightened, his breath coming in short pants as if something...or someone...had reversed the effects of the sedatives.

"Down, boy," I said to Chaos as I pried Jason's grip from my arm and stepped away. His expression immediately returned to a vacant stare. "Thank you for talking to us."

Ember followed me to the door, her face solemn. "You were right," she said as she pulled the door shut. "The demon drew them there. A witch who didn't understand magic was in the wrong place at the wrong time, and three people are dead because of it."

I nodded. "And I highly doubt she had the power to summon Discord."

"Which means we're back to square one, with no clue who started this mess."

"Cinder had a clue."

Ember looked at me sideways as we paced down the hall.

"She had the sigils in her room," I said. "It can't be a coincidence." We exited the building and climbed into the van.

"I hear you." Ember started the engine and backed out of her parking space. "But whatever clue she had; she took it with her."

"Maybe not." I rubbed my palms on my jeans. "I found her diary under the mattress with the sigils."

She slammed on the brakes. "And you're just now telling me about this?"

"I tried to talk to you about it last night, but you shut me down. The page of demon symbols was inside one of my sigil books, and that book was lying next to her diary."

She looked at me like I'd grown horns. "What did it say?"

I ran my fingers through my hair to make sure I hadn't. Whew. No horns. "I didn't read it."

"Why not? It could have clues to what happened to her. To Mom and Dad."

I held up my hands. "First off, it has her private thoughts. There might be stuff in there we don't want to know, and I'm not in the habit of snooping. Second, I was a little distracted by the demon in my head and then the one in the woods. It's in my desk drawer."

"If she did summon my brother with his skull, she might have known where mine is."

I hated to admit it, but it was in everyone's best interest for us to peruse Cinder's private thoughts. I sighed. "We'll read it when we get home."

"Oh, hell." Ember rolled to a stop on South Washington Square, bordering Salem Common, an eight-acre park in the heart of downtown. "Can we not make it from point A to point B without a fiasco?"

She grabbed her phone and pressed it to her ear while I peered out the window at the commotion. People screamed, throwing their arms over their heads and running for cover. A black mass followed a man who darted toward the gazebo, a stray blob freeing itself from the herd to latch onto his neck. He swatted it away, and it hit the ground before rising and rejoining the mass.

"Is that a swarm of fae?" I crawled over the console, into the backseat to retrieve my spell kit. Crap. I never had time to restock it.

"Sure looks like it. Shade is on his way. Can you slow the critters down until they get here?" She pulled off the road and parked in a no-parking zone. Chief Higgins would make the ticket disappear if need be. He owed us that much.

"There is a rift here. I can sense it."

"No shit, Sherlock." I balanced the bowl on the back seat and dumped in the ingredients for my newly concocted spell. "Stray fae get through here and there year-round, but I've never encountered a swarm that big."

"I despise the fae."

"Don't we all?" Their high-pitched laughs were enough to drive anyone mad, but those teeth... Tiny, razor-sharp daggers filled their mouths, and they loved the taste of human blood. They were the mosquitos of my nightmares.

Ember exited the driver's side and opened the back door. "No talking to Chaos when the other witches are around. The demon business is between you and me for now. If no one has a hostile takeover planned yet, they will when they find out you performed dark magic."

Way to blame it all on me, sis. Then again, she wasn't wrong.

"It was an accident, but I get it. I was afraid to even tell you." I made twice as much potion as last time. I might need to slow the onlookers down too, so they didn't get too close to the faeries.

"I'm glad you did." She strapped her sword to her back and attached two daggers to her thighs before gripping my arm. "Hey. You know you can tell me anything, right?"

"I know." I forced a smile, and she let me go. I'd always been closer to Cinder. Ember and I got along just fine, but when I had a secret to share, I went to Cinder. Em was trying to fill that void for me. The least I could do was give back a little.

"You know what's weird? I'm not scared of Chaos. You'd think being possessed would be the most frightening thing ever, but it's not. I think he kinda likes me."

His deep chuckle reverberated through me. *"I can think of worse witches to be trapped inside."*

She scrunched her nose. "You're right. That is weird."

See why I always confided in Cinder? I dropped the spearmint oil into the mixture, activating it, and poured the granules into my hand. "I hope Shade is close. I don't know how long this spell lasts."

"He was ten minutes out."

I nodded and climbed out of the van. My boots crunched on the fallen leaves as I marched toward the faeries and shouted, "Hey! Your main course is here."

Did I mention they loved witch blood even more than human?

The swarm flew toward me, and the onlookers gasped. One of the little suckers broke free from the brood and nipped at my neck, taking a chunk of skin with it. That was a lucky shot; it wouldn't happen again. Did I also mention how much I hated faeries?

I bent down, pretending to scoop a handful of dirt, and threw it into the fray. Their velocity slowed until they appeared to be flying through invisible mud, their little brown wings flapping in slow motion.

"What in the world?" a man asked, and people gathered around, a new swarm, just as dangerous as the first, descending on me.

Glad I made a double spell. I whispered the incantation, putting as much of my vim into it as I dared before tossing the granules in a circular motion, making a ring around the area. It didn't fill all eight acres—how could it?—but hopefully it slowed their thoughts down too or the humans would have a slew of conspiracy theories when this was through.

Now if Shade would get his ass here, we could hide this from the rest of the town, I could locate the rift and close it, and we could be on our way. I dropped my spell bag on the ground and squatted next to it before preparing the perimeter location potion. Thankfully, I still had all the ingredients for this one.

Restocking would be at the top of my to-do list as soon as we got home.

Along with reading Cinder's journal, finding Chaos's skull, exorcizing him, finding Cinder... I was giving myself anxiety just thinking about the length of that list.

I crushed the herbs in the bowl, and the energy around me shifted. Everything took on a grayish tinge, like I was looking through fog.

"It's about damn time." I glanced up at Shade before continuing my potion. He'd brought Ginger and Miles along too. "They're just a few fae. You didn't have to bring the calvary." I dropped in the final ingredient, and the mixture smoked before turning to fine powder.

Shade stepped toward the swarm and poked a faery. Its mouth opened slowly as if it were trying to snap at his finger. "What the hell kind of magic is this? I've never seen this spell before."

"It's experimental. I made it on the fly when we fought the demon, and it worked for that." I stood and poured the powdered spell into my palm.

He curled his lip. "Would have been more efficient to freeze them."

I fisted my hand around the powder, fighting the urge to test the hardness of his jaw with my knuckles. "I didn't have the right ingredients, or I would have."

He clicked his tongue. "Some girl scout you are,

running into a fight unprepared. If I were you, I'd have premixed binding and perimeter locators on hand." He swept his gaze across the Common. "Where's the rift? I suppose you need me to seal it too?"

Who was worse? The fae or Shade? I wasn't sure. Would it be awful of me to shove him through the rift once I found it? Maybe a little.

"The only reason I couldn't close it before was because I had fought a *demon*. When was the last time you battled a creature from Hell?" I brushed past him, said the incantation, and blew the powder into the air. Like last time, it turned to fog and rolled through the grounds until it met the rift.

Ember stood next to me, facing the others. "Round up the little buggers and shove them through. Ash and I will seal it."

Chaos growled in my head. *"I don't like the way he talks to you."*

I turned and walked with her toward the rift. "Shade is an ass."

"I heard that!" He plucked a faery from the bunch and examined it.

"Good," I shouted back without turning around.

"Your High Priestess should protect you from him."

I laughed and lowered my voice. "I don't need protection from Shade. He's all bark and no bite."

Ember shot me a warning look. "Where's your earbud?"

"Sorry. I'll be quiet." I slipped my bag off my shoulder and rummaged through it while Ginger shoved an armful of fae through the rift.

"Here." Miles held a vial toward me, his gray eyes shifting as he spoke. "Shade asked me to make a few to keep on hand in case it happened again."

I pressed my lips together, wanting ever so badly to refuse his offer for the simple fact that Shade had commissioned the potion. I was loath to use my vim with his intentions, but it would speed things along.

"Thanks." I accepted it, but I want it noted how reluctant I was. Also, Miles was the new guy. Sure, he was great at spells, but why would Shade have commissioned them from him? Probably to turn him against me. The dipshit.

"How do these creatures survive in a realm infested with demons and ghouls?" Shade asked as he sent an armful through the tear. "Seems like they'd be easy pickings."

"The other realm has multiple layers, like this one. Much like spirits can linger here undetected in a separate plane, the fae exist in their own level of the realm. Demons have their own space, but they can freely cross the layers."

I paraphrased what he said.

"That makes sense." Ember gave me the look again, reminding me not to reveal the voice in my head.

Shade narrowed his eyes. "Why do you know so much about demons?"

"Because I read." I crossed my arms. "You should try cracking a book sometime."

With the last of the fae on the correct side of the veil, I popped the top on the brew and took Ember's hand. "Fabric torn will be reborn. Seal these treads so we don't end up dead."

Shade scoffed behind me, no doubt expecting my incantation to fail, but I ignored him like the adult I was supposed to be.

I poured the mixture over the rip, and the treads shone gold as they stitched themselves back together. "Thanks for that," I whispered before giving Ember's hand a squeeze and letting go.

"Anytime." She turned toward the others. "Great work today. Thanks for getting here on such short notice."

"Are you going to call a meeting to talk about why this keeps happening?" Ginger asked.

Ember shook her head. "Not yet. I have some more research to do."

"A group brainstorming session would be beneficial," Shade said. "The more ideas we have, the faster we'll find the problem and fix it."

"I bet it's something on the other side," Miles said. "Maybe the fae are organizing. They aren't all mindless bloodsuckers like these."

Ember cut her gaze to me before speaking. "We're working on it. Give us some time."

"But..." Shade started to argue, but Ember lifted her hand.

"Go home before the humans get unstuck," she said. "Bottle some spells for freezing monsters and sealing the veil. If you can, bottle some of your shadow work for us to carry when you aren't around. I know it won't be as powerful, but it'll help in cases like this."

He nodded. "Okay. Keep us informed."

"Will do," Ember said, and we headed for the van.

When we got home, I carried in my travel spell kit to restock it. No way was I using someone else's spell again. Especially one from Shade. I needed to soak in a tub of hand sanitizer and hyssop in a bathroom full of sage and drink a gallon of basil and patchouli tea to clear his ick from my body and soul. I shuddered and set the bag on the kitchen counter.

Ember gripped my shoulder. "Are you okay? Is the demon...?"

"I'm fine. Chaos has been quiet since we left the Common. I just..." I lined the empty bottles next to the bag and opened the pantry. "Why did you tell Shade to make the freezing and sealing spells? You know I can make them. It's literally *my job* to supply you with whatever you need to hunt monsters."

She slid onto a stool across the counter. "I'm sorry.

I was trying to get him off our backs so we could figure things out."

I dumped an armful of herbs next to the bottles. "Shadow magic, okay. He's the only one in the coven with that kind of power, so sure. Ask him to bottle that, but don't take away one of the few ways I can contribute to solving the problem."

A growl rumbled in my head. *"You shouldn't let such an insignificant little man affect your emotions like this. You are a Holland witch. He is nothing."*

"I know." I sighed heavily and refilled the peppermint oil. "I'm working on it."

"When you find my skull and free me, I'll see to it that he never bothers you again."

I laughed. "Thanks. Wait... What do you mean by that?"

"What would you like? I can drive him mad with a touch, or if you prefer, I can tear him limb from limb before dragging him to Hell. I haven't decided which would be a better punishment for the way he treats you."

"Absolutely not!" It was tempting, but no. I grabbed a big copper bowl and my mortar and pestle from the cabinet.

"What's he saying?" Ember asked.

"He's telling me all the things he could do to Shade once he's free."

Her brows crept toward her hairline.

"He won't. Will you, Chaos?"

"I make no promises."

I fisted my hands on my hips. "Well, you better start. You will not harm a coven member. Understood?"

"Understood. I won't...unless you ask me to."

I fought a grin and looked at Ember. "He's a demon. He's got to learn the way we do things around here."

She rolled her eyes. "You mean passive-aggressive jabs and pissing contests as often as possible?"

"Exactly." I set the rest of my supplies on the counter.

"Where's the journal?"

"In my desk drawer downstairs."

"You could've grabbed it before we came up," she grumbled as she headed to the library.

"Yeah, well..." I dumped the ingredients for the sealing spell into the bowl. This whole ordeal was a giant shit show. I'd summoned a friggin' demon, for Hecate's sake, and there was a good chance Cinder...our former acting High Priestess...had summoned one too. Salem was turning into total chaos with all these tears in the veil...that the Holland witches were apparently responsible for, and Shade just had to one-up me every chance he got.

Oh, and now the asshat was in the process of turning Miles against me. And with Miles would go

Ginger too. She was super nice to me now, but she and Miles were dating, so...

"Whoa," Ember said as she froze in the kitchen entrance. "What's gotten into you? It looks like a tornado tore through the place."

"What?" I snapped before glancing around the room. Holy mother of magic. Loose herbs littered the countertop, and my orderly line of bottles was now scattered across the room. Some lay on the floor while others rolled across the opposite counter. A box of baking soda had fallen open on the tile, and footprints —my footprints—tracked from the pantry to the sink to the place I currently stood.

"What the hell?" Ground sage coated my hands, so I paced to the sink and rinsed it off. I didn't remember doing any of this. That could only mean one thing... "Chaos?"

A full three seconds passed before he answered. *"Yes."*

"Yes? That's all you have to say?" I picked up the strewn bottles and lined them up again before getting a dustpan after the rest of the mess. Ember returned to her stool and laid the journal in front of her.

"I'm trying not to take over, but our souls are melding. You're the epitome of order. That's the only reason you've been able to resist my nature for so long."

"For so long? A day and a half is long?"

Ember pinned me with a steely gaze. "What's going on? Did Chaos make you do this?"

"You need to tell her."

"The hell I do." I scrubbed the counter with a disinfecting wipe.

"Stop!" Ember slapped her hand on top of mine, stilling me. "I want to help get this demon out of your head, but I need to know what's going on. I'm only hearing one side of your dialogue, so you need to explain it to me."

I sucked in a deep breath and tried to slide my hand out from under hers. She tightened her grip. "It's not important. Let's just read the journal and see if Cinder mentioned anything about finding a skull."

"It is important. I have never seen you make a mess in your entire life. Even as a toddler, you were organizing your toys more than playing with them."

"Tell her."

"Okay. Fine." I pulled my hand again, but she didn't let go. Cocking my head, I gave her a hard look, and she finally released me. "You've got so much shit on your plate right now; I didn't want to worry you."

She folded her hands on top of the journal. "Worry me, Ash. Please."

"It's..." I drummed my nails on the counter twice. "Chaos can't stay in my head forever."

"Obviously."

"His consciousness is kinda melding with mine,

and if I don't send him packing soon, he'll sorta take over." I shrugged and returned to my cleaning.

Her mouth formed a straight line. "Say that again without the qualifiers."

I huffed. "His consciousness is melding with mine, and if I don't get him out soon, he'll take over."

She leaned on her forearms. "This is serious, Ash."

"I know it is. That's why I didn't want to tell you." I dumped the contents of the mixing bowl into the trash. Who knew what I'd thrown in there during my chaotic blackout?

"How long do you have?"

"I don't know. Chaos?"

"With your immense power, no more than two weeks."

I looked at Ember. "Two weeks, tops. Read the journal while I restock the kit. It's our best bet for fixing all this."

My sister scanned the pages while I made another batch of sealing potion. Thankfully, Chaos stayed quiet and didn't turn me into Hurricane Ash again. Ember gasped a few times, and I tried to ignore the growing expression of alarm widening her eyes as she absorbed whatever Cinder had written.

She swallowed audibly and looked up from the pages. "Holy Hecate. The curse, Ash. You didn't break the curse by surviving. You *are* the curse."

TEN

The blood in my head plummeted to my feet. I held onto the counter and slowly made my way around to Ember. "What do you mean, I *am* the curse? What does it say?"

"She knew you would find it. Cinder knew you'd detect the spell."

I clenched my teeth. "What does it say?"

She let out a slow breath and opened the journal to the first page. "'Dear Ash. If you're reading this, I never made it back.'" She pushed the book toward me. "Do you want to read it?"

I shook my head and sank onto the stool next to her, a sense of dread tightening my stomach, making me feel like I'd swallowed a brick.

Ember nodded and continued reading aloud. "'I

know you planned to organize the library in Dad's absence, so I hid your favorite sigil book next to this journal in hopes that you'd find it should I go missing too. I really did leave in search of our parents. I didn't lie about that, but there are other things you need to know. You and Ember.' Hold on. I need a drink. Want one?"

I swallowed the dryness from my mouth. "Sure."

Ember grabbed two beers from the fridge and popped the tops before returning to her seat. She took a long pull from her bottle and slid mine toward me. The icy bubbles loosened the thickness in my throat, but they did nothing to quell the sense of impending doom churning in my gut. Chaos hadn't said a word, which was a very, very bad sign.

"'Our parents lied to you about the curse. They lied to us all. Every High Priestess that came before Mom lied too. You aren't the miracle baby she made you out to be. There's a reason why you're the only third daughter to survive. Mom didn't have the heart to kill you.'"

My eyes blinked rapidly of their own accord. I took another swig of beer, but it barely made it past my throat.

Ember continued, "'The curse wasn't that every third daughter of the High Priestess would die in infancy. It was that she would go insane and murder everyone in the coven.'"

"Wait. What?" No way would I murder the coven. I loved our coven and most of the people in it. "That can't be right."

Ember gave me a sympathetic look and read some more. "'I know it's hard to believe, but mom showed me the curse. It was in the dark grimoire in the safe.'"

I shot to my feet. "This can't be happening. I need to see it for myself."

"Hold on." Ember grabbed my wrist and tugged me back into my seat. "You need to hear the rest of this first. 'The dirty secret of our coven is that if the High Priestess has a third daughter, she murders her. It has happened several times over the centuries, and the knowledge about the real curse is passed orally from the High Priestess to her oldest daughter. That's why I now know.'"

Holy mother of magic and mayhem. What the actual eff? "I've got a demon inside me. Chaos, are you the reason I'm supposedly going to murder my coven? Are you going to force me to do it?"

Five seconds passed before he responded. *"You have my word that I will not force you to murder your coven. The only person in danger from this possession is you."*

"What about after? When you take over completely?"

"I thought the plan was to find my skull so that won't happen."

"But if we don't?" My voice trembled, hysteria edging my words.

"*If we don't, no more harm will come to your coven. I promise.*"

That should have relieved me a little, but it didn't. "He says it won't be because of him. What else did Cinder say?"

"'Mom has been searching for a way to break the curse since you were born. She was certain she'd figured out how to end it for good without harming you. The witch who hexed us harnessed the power of three demons, and only three demons can break the curse.

'Mom and Dad went into the woods to summon one. They cut a deal with him. I overheard them talking about it. They promised their souls in exchange for him delivering the fiends responsible. The demon required the grimoire, so they took it back to the woods, but the one they bargained with was a trickster. He took the book and our parents, but not before I tore out the page identifying the only demons who could break the curse. The ones who created it.'"

I opened my mouth to speak, but whatever words I thought I had to say got stuck in my throat. The page of sigils that had fallen out of my book. I had possessed myself with the same demon who cursed my bloodline.

"Chaos..." I said, my jaw clenched.

Silence answered me.

"There's more," Ember said. "'The one who cursed us moved to Boston and joined the Magic Society there. I broke into their library, and that's where I discovered what she had done. She had promised her own soul and her firstborn's in exchange for the power, but she never planned to hold up her end of the deal.

'She vanquished the three demon brothers but hid their skulls. Without their bodies intact, they can't reform in Hell. They're trapped in a dark prison, and never got to collect her soul. The only way to break the curse is for us to release them. They are the only ones who can help.'"

"Chaos!" I shouted, and Ember jumped. "Is this true? Did you curse my family?"

One second. Two seconds. Three seconds. "*My brothers and I let the witch use our power, yes.*"

"But you said if I went insane, it wouldn't be because of you. Liar." My hands curled into tight fists, and my heart rate kicked into a sprint.

"*No, you said it wouldn't be because of me. I said I wouldn't murder your coven or make you do it while in possession.*"

I crossed my arms. "Lying by omission is still lying."

"I'm a demon." I could almost see his nonchalant shrug.

"That's no excuse, mister." I jabbed my finger forward as if he were in front of me. "You have to fix this. I can't murder my entire coven."

My sister arched a brow. "Are you done?"

"Not yet. Did you know about this all along, demon boy?" I fumed. How could he betray me like this?

"I have known since you told me you were a Holland and the youngest of three."

I sucked in a breath to berate him more, but he continued, *"If you want to save your coven, you have two options. Find our skulls and release us. We will be in your debt, and I will try to convince my brothers to release you from the curse in exchange for our freedom."*

Sure. That sounded like an easy task. Not. "And option two?"

"Allow me to take over. Give your life to me, cease to exist. Without you, your coven is safe...until the next third-born daughter arises."

I told Ember what he said.

"Let me guess," she scoffed. "He suggests the second option."

"While that would be the easier of the two, my brother would still be imprisoned, and you would no longer exist. The world is a better place with you in it."

"Is that so?" I rolled my eyes. "He votes for option

one. Release him and his brothers, break the curse, and we can all be done with each other for good."

"I didn't say..."

"What?" I snapped.

"Nothing. Does Cinder mention if she found Discord's skull?"

I looked at Ember. "Did she write anything else?"

"I wondered if you were ever going to let me finish. 'I've located Discord's skull, and I'm going to release him. I'll convince him to take me into Hell so I can find Mom and Dad. I hope to bring them back right away, so you never have to read this, but if I don't return, you have to release the other two. We can end this. I know we can.'"

"Does she say where she found the skull?"

"Anything else? A treasure map with X marks the spot for the other skulls?"

Ember shook her head. "Nothing. The rest of the pages are blank."

"Well, crappity crap." My shoulders slumped. "What now?"

Ember drummed her fingers on the counter. "Cinder got the intel about the skulls from the Boston Magic Society's library. Sounds to me like another break-in is in order."

I choked on my beer. "You want to break into a dark witch coven's library? Are you insane? Do you know how many boobytraps they'll have set? I wouldn't be surprised if they have magical acid to burn our faces off Indiana Jones-style."

She lifted one shoulder dismissively. "Cinder pulled it off. Why can't we?"

"Because she's *Cinder*, the most powerful witch in our coven, if not in all of Massachusetts."

"*Actually—*"

"Oh no." I held up a finger. "Don't you 'actually' me, mister. You're in no position to demonsplain. I'm putting you in a timeout."

"*But—*"

"Nope."

"*If you'll—*"

"Zip it."

He growled, but he didn't say any more. Good boy. Once I got him out of my head, I'd have to teach him to sit.

Ember tossed her empty bottle into the recycle bin. "I'll humor you. Cinder may be the most powerful witch in the coven on her own, but you and I together are a force to be reckoned with. We've already vanquished a demon and a swarm of fae. We've got this."

"Do we?" I got nauseated even considering this suggestion, but... "Maybe if we had Shade, we could pull it off, but you and me alone...?" My body shuddered in revulsion. I despised that man way more than necessary, but I couldn't help it.

"We can't involve him."

Thank the goddess. "I agree one hundred percent."

"We can't let anyone know about this. A light witch consorting with demons is grounds for banishment. A family member of the High Priestess doing it could mean our family losing control of the coven. Add to that the fact they've been lied to about the curse for centuries, and... Cinder will bring our parents back. We owe it to them to keep the coven under control."

I scrunched my nose. "We do have a very good reason for consorting with these particular demons. Maybe we could enlist one other monster hunter. Someone who can fight... Just in case."

"You can fight, Ash."

I laughed dryly. "I can also accidentally set their headquarters on fire."

"Spells, sis. Sigils and spells are your weapons. Forget about the fire."

My teeth clicked together. *Forget about the fire*, she said to the freaking fire witch. I knew she meant well, but I couldn't lie. That comment stung.

"You can do this. Your coven and your life depend on it."

Ember clasped her hands beneath her chin and flashed a fake smile. "What do you say, dear sister?"

My nostrils flared as I blew out a long, slow breath. I was supposed to be the voice of reason.

Ember was the impulsive one. I tried to talk her out of her worst decisions. But at this point, I didn't see any other way. I mean, aside from letting Chaos take over my body, burn it up, and turn it into his own.

Hecate help me. "I say we're breaking into the Boston coven library."

CHAPTER

ELEVEN

A chill that had nothing to do with the weather crept up my spine as Ember and I silently slid out of the van and gathered our gear. Thick clouds blanketed the sky, too high to be rain clouds but ominous enough to add to the foreboding feeling tying my insides into knots.

We'd parked in an alley four blocks from the Boston Magic Society's headquarters, and thank the goddess it wasn't raining. Wet leather chafed like a mother effer. I needed to work on a spell to fix that. Fireproofing had been my initial goal—Ember relied on it so her clothes didn't char and fall off every time she fought a monster—but an end to the chafing was next on my list.

Ember strapped her sword onto her back and secured daggers on her thighs and ankles. She looked like a total badass, as usual. I slung the magic kit crossways on my shoulder and checked to be sure my boots were tied.

"Here. Take this, just in case." My sister shoved a six-inch, sheathed dagger toward me, complete with leather straps to wrap around my thigh.

"You said no one would be there." I accepted the weapon and attached the scabbard to my leg. Better safe than sorry.

"It's the Hunter's Moon tonight. They'll be in the Boston Common performing their annual ritual. Dark magic practitioners hold this full moon above all others."

I narrowed my eyes. "And you don't think they'll leave anyone behind as guard? They can't even trust their own people."

"Mm-mm. Remember those boobytraps you were worried about? It's your job to nullify them without setting off the alarm. I'll do the rest."

"Fabulous."

Headlights approached from the cross street, and Ember flattened herself against the van. "You've got Shade's spells?"

My lip curled. "Yeah."

"Good. Activate one to get us from here to there. Be ready for the second one when it wears off."

I stuck my finger into my mouth, pretending to gag.

Ember rolled her eyes. "Real mature, Ash."

"His intentions just don't mix well with my vim. We're like oil and water. Colors that clash. Eating a greasy burrito on a transatlantic flight."

The car passed, and she slid the door shut. "Then why did you sleep with him?"

"I..." My mouth hung open as I tried to find the words to defend myself.

"You had sex with the man you despise?" Chaos sounded incredulous, and I couldn't say I blamed him. I sometimes had trouble believing it myself.

"There was alcohol involved. Alcohol leads to bad decisions. I know it was wrong." In my defense, I had just finished a fabulous enemies-to-lovers romance novel, and I was still caught up in the magic of my favorite trope. A lower-level demon had slipped through the veil, as they did in Salem from time to time, and the team had vanquished it. No ghoul guts or cemetery fires involved.

Tequila shots in the kitchen to celebrate. Ember went to bed; everyone else went home. Shade stayed. You can figure out the rest. I woke up with regrets; he woke with goo-goo eyes. Cocky asshats didn't handle rejection well. We went from mildly annoying each other to mortal enemies in one night flat.

"Did he force you? I'll tear off his limbs and shove them into every orifice on his body."

Now that would be a sight to see. "Down, boy. Nobody forced anybody. It was a mutual mistake."

"You set?" Ember's voice pulled me to the present.

"Ready as I'll ever be to sneak into a booby-trapped, dark magic HQ." Which was not at all.

"Activate the first shadow spell."

I really did gag a little this time, but I tried my best to hide it as I popped the cork on Shade's bottled essence—double gag—and poured the black powder into my hand. Then I read the slip of paper he'd included with the vials. "Hide from sight our magical plight. With the power of Shade, my intent is conveyed."

Seriously? Who wrote themselves into a spell? I was certain he rhymed it that way just to grate on my nerves. Whatever.

I blew the power into the air, and it billowed into a thick gray cloud before falling around us, cloaking us. The world turned unsaturated, nearly grayscale, and we hoofed it toward the entrance.

Okay, that wasn't so bad. Maybe I had been a bit overly dramatic about using shadow magic. Note to self: act like an effing grownup. Especially when he was poking me. Metaphorically, of course, because his poker would never get close enough to poke me again.

Two blocks from our target, a homeless man sat huddled against a building. A little brown terrier lay beside him, snuggled in a green blanket while the man used a piece of a cardboard box to block the wind. My heart ached for the pair, so I dug in my pocket and pulled out a ten.

He didn't react as I approached, and when I laid the money on the ground next to him, he sucked in a ragged breath, his hooded eyes growing wide like saucers. "A blessing from the goddess," he mumbled.

I smiled. "Something like that."

"Ash!" Ember shouted. "No time for bleeding hearts. Let's keep moving."

The man tucked the money into his shirt, completely oblivious to our presence.

"The spell mutes sound too?" I followed my sister across the intersection. The building stood one block away.

"I told him to put everything he had into them. He'll probably sleep fifteen hours tonight. He looked like shit when I picked them up."

"Well, color me impressed."

"Me too. Maybe I won't kill him. He seems useful to you."

I laughed. "I suppose he can be."

Ember lifted her brows, silently telling me to fill her in.

"He says Shade might be useful, so he won't kill him."

"Probably won't."

She crossed her arms, widening her stance. "If he

so much as pretends he's going to harm one of our coven members, I'll send him right back to his dark prison and turn his skull into powder so he can never resurrect."

"I would like to see her try."

I held up my hands. "Stop, both of you. Let's focus on the mission, mm-kay? My heart is beating like a racehorse trampling through my chest, and I would like to get this over with before they get done with their ritual."

"Hmph," he grumbled.

"Right back at ya, dude," I said.

Ember parked a hand on her hip. "I'm not kidding."

"He already promised not to hurt anyone in the coven." I pulled another shadow spell from my satchel and popped it open...without cringing, I might add.

With our cover reinforced, we crept toward the three-story brick building. The racehorse in my chest kicked into overdrive, and I sucked in a deep breath, hoping to slow it before I hyperventilated.

"This is as close as I'm willing to get until we know what kind of magic is protecting the place. Do your thing, sis." Ember motioned toward the front door.

"Here we go." I kept the kit stocked with individual ingredients so the hunters could make whatever spells they needed on the fly. This time, I had an idea of what we'd be up against, so I'd packed a slew of ready-made potions.

This spell, however, was a specialty of mine. I'd practiced it so much I didn't need the help of a potion. Being the youngest, I'd used it plenty of times to snoop in my sisters' rooms, finding all the charms they'd put up to hide things. "Confess, expose my magic sleuth. I call on you to reveal your truth."

I directed my intention toward the door and the nearby windows. Gold sparkled in the air, looking for signs of magic, but it fell to the ground, dissipating. Huh. That was odd.

"No magic on the entrance?" Ember asked.

"Doesn't appear that way." I crept up the stairs and tried the handle. "Just a lock."

Chaos growled in my head.

"What?" I asked.

"*There's magic inside. Dark magic obtained from my realm.*"

"Of course there is. They're a dark magic coven. It's kinda their thing." I dug a lock-picking kit from my satchel and kneeled in front of the door.

"*It's too dangerous. You should wait until I'm free so I can take out the coven. Then you can access all their knowledge without risking your life.*"

"There's a problem with your plan. Two, actually." I slid the tension wrench into the bottom of the keyhole and applied a little pressure. "We don't *take out* other covens. They're not a group of serial killers. They're a bunch of self-serving witches who like to stir up trouble in their own town. Not our problem. They don't mess with us, and we don't report them to the Higher Power."

"Is he trying to convince you to kill them all?" Concern creased Ember's forehead.

"He's afraid we're going to get hurt." I slid the rake in above the wrench and scrubbed it in a circular motion, disengaging the pins one by one.

"Better them than you."

"Problem two: I can't free you without *accessing their knowledge,* so zip it and let me get us inside before the shadow spell wears off." I fought a grin. I hated to admit it, but it was kinda sweet that this big, growly demon was concerned for my safety.

Wait a minute. Demons weren't sweet.

"Why do you even care? If I do nothing, you get to take over in a couple of weeks. You'll be free whether I live or not."

He missed several beats as he formulated his reply. For a demon named Chaos, he sure had a lot of control. *"I am in your debt, and..."* Another beat. Make that two. *"You deserve life."*

The lock disengaged, and I shoved the tools into my satchel. "We're in." I tapped the door with my finger, making sure it wasn't going to blow off the hinges at the first creak. It swung freely, so I stepped back and directed another magic-revealing spell into the opening. Again, no enchantments protected the entrance.

"This doesn't feel right." I rose to my feet, but my stomach didn't go up with the rest of me. It continued sinking into my boots. "A human could have picked this lock. I know the BMS isn't an ethical coven, but they'd protect their assets from the mundane if only to cover their asses with the Higher Power."

"The shadow spell is wearing off, so make a decision. I'm going in." Ember strode past me with the confidence of a gazelle walking into a pride of lions. Sure, she could outmaneuver them, but she was oblivious to their strength. Typical Ember.

I slung the satchel over my shoulder and followed her inside, closing the door behind me. Ember lit a fireball in her hand, and I shined a flashlight around the room. Ah. This made sense. The front of their HQ was a witchy shop like ours. If a mundane wanted to rob it, they couldn't have them bursting into flames the second they stepped inside.

I blew out the breath I was well aware I'd been holding. Temptation to see if they sold any actual spells in their shop had me itching to check the place out, but Ember's impatient glare as she stood by the door leading deeper into their lair kept my curiosity in check.

"What lies beyond that threshold can kill you."

"I figured as much." A quick test with my trusty gold sparkles revealed an electrification spell. I tilted my head and watched the glitter cling to the fabric of the enchantment. "This layer of protection has been here a long time. See how it's rooted to the floor and door frame?"

I gestured to show Ember how the fibers thickened where the layer of magic connected to the building. "They must all have tokens that allow them to pass through unharmed."

She unsheathed her sword. "Can you unravel it gently, or do I get to tear it apart?"

"I've got this." The last thing I needed was for Ember to get electrocuted and leave me alone with whatever beastie they might have guarding the place.

I snatched two black tourmaline pendants from the rack and rubbed them with horehound leaves. After a quick incantation, they glowed blue before fading back to their normal hue. We slipped the cords around our necks and eyed the deadly door.

I took a step back. "If this doesn't work, we'll be Kentucky fried and dead on the floor."

"Do you think it'll work?" She flicked her gaze to me before focusing on the electric field blocking our way.

"It should. Unless…"

"Good enough for me." Ember stepped through the door without even an arm hair standing on end.

My stomach clenched along with my jaw, my hands fisting instinctively. One of these days, her gall would get her killed. Hopefully this would not be that day.

"This was genius, Ash," Ember whispered. "We can get in and out without them knowing we were here."

"That's the plan." I stepped in behind her.

"Good luck with that."

"Thanks for the vote of confidence."

Chaos grunted. *"Can you not feel the demonic magic in the air?"*

"Nope." I shined my flashlight around the room. A long rectangular table took up the center of the space, with chairs crammed around all the sides. At the head of the table loomed an ornate...I could only call it a throne, with gilded edges and intricate dark magic carvings.

"Stop and try. It's unmistakable."

Ember curled her lip. "A little pretentious, isn't it? Their archives must be farther back." She gestured at the door, waiting for me to check it for magic.

"Hold on." I took a deep breath and focused on the energy in the air. It felt sticky, like the magic performed there wasn't always done with good intentions. Obviously, or they wouldn't be a dark magic coven. "What am I looking for?"

"The lowest vibration you've ever felt. It will penetrate your flesh and hum in your bones. Concentrate."

"Let's go, Ash." Ember jerked her head toward the door.

"Wait. He's teaching me how to sense demon magic. It could come in handy." I closed my eyes and let all the energy in the room wash over me. I'd need an insanely hot shower when this was through. Sticky, icky remnants of dark magic clung to my skin, but something *other* engulfed me too.

Like Chaos described, the vibration was lower, slower than anything I'd felt before and it did indeed penetrate all the way to my bones, giving me the same pins and needles sensation as when your foot falls asleep, but much, *much* deeper.

"Holy Hecate. Is this what your presence will feel like once you're out of my head?"

"Mine and every demon you encounter. Proceed with caution."

"Always." I joined my sister at the next doorway and activated the magic-revealing spell. "This one isn't protected."

"Probably because of what's waiting for us inside." Ember clutched her sword in both hands and crept down the staircase.

My flashlight penetrated the darkness, revealing a long corridor that slanted even farther downward. We were headed deep into the basement, and I could guarantee the door leading to the surface outside would be protected with something even more potent than the electricity spell cloaking the inside door. I had no idea if our crystals would shield us from it, which meant we had one way of escape if things went south. Back the way we came.

I said a quick prayer to the goddess that things would stay above the equator.

The corridor spilled out into a massive, stone-lined room, and silence engulfed us. The musty scent of old books, which usually brought me a sense of peace, smelled more like rot and clay. Not a single window lined the wall near the ceiling to let in an ounce of light. We must've been too deep.

I swept the beam along the wall, illuminating a switch attached to a silver plate. Metal tubing ran up the surface and across the ceiling toward a massive chandelier. I flipped the switch.

Lights from sconces added to the brilliant chande-lier bulbs, revealing a library so massive I couldn't hide my envy. My mouth dropped open as I took in rows and rows of shelving units so tall they had wheeled ladders attached to each one. "Whoa."

"Wow." Even Ember was in awe. "They have twice as many books as us. How are we going to find anything?"

I chuckled. "I'll tell you how." A card catalog stood right in front of us, gleaming in the warm light, dark cherry wood housing columns of five-inch drawers with golden handles. One day, my library would be this organized. Maybe not as flashy and big, but it would be awesome.

"Ash?"

"Mm-hmm?" I slid out a drawer and ran my fingers over the cards, a smile tugging at my lips.

"Have you forgotten about the demon guarding this place?"

Honestly? Yeah, I had forgotten. The library was nothing short of magnificent.

"Oh shit." Ember backed into me, ramming me into the catalog. The drawer slammed shut on my finger, and I yanked it out, sticking it in my mouth as if that would ease the smashing pain.

"Find the info fast," she said over her shoulder. "I'll take care of the beastie."

I spun around and nearly peed my pants. An eight-foot creature with a massive jaw and fangs that belonged on a sabertooth tiger prowled toward her, and it was entirely made of clay.

So that was what I smelled.

CHAPTER

TWELVE

"Here, demon, demon." Ember made a come get me motion with her hand and crept off to the right. The fiend grunted at me, looked at her, and lunged. Smart move for the demon; bad news for me. He planned to take out the most dangerous threat first so he could toy with the weaker one. Yay.

She stabbed her sword right into his gut and twisted before yanking it out. He stumbled, but the clay reformed, filling in the gash within seconds. "Does this library have advice on how to kill a golem?" she asked.

Chaos growled. *"Being trapped in a golem is almost as bad as the prison you rescued me from. He is their slave and will do their bidding until he is released."*

"And I guess their bidding is to protect their secrets at all costs. How do we release him?"

"Only the one who trapped him can."

"Fabulous. Hey, Em? He can't be killed, so just keep him busy while I find the book."

"Challenge accepted." She spun in a circle and swiped her sword, taking his arm off at the elbow. I was about to say one point for Ember, but a new arm formed where she'd cut him, and the one on the floor turned to goo, rolled across the concrete, and attached itself to his leg.

"That's not fair." Ember backed up, drawing the golem farther away from me. I had a feeling she'd never fought one of these before, so she'd either have the time of her life or end up dead. The faster I could find the book, the more likely it would be the former.

I yanked open the drawer with the letter D and flipped to the cards about demons. "Frickity frak. There must be a hundred entries." A quick glance at the drawers below confirmed it. There were three D drawers.

"How about curses?" The C drawer wasn't much better. At least fifty volumes held information about curses. "I would appreciate any advice you could give me, Chaos." Because I was getting nowhere, which meant bad news for my sister.

She grunted, and I looked up in time to see her fly

backward and smack into a bookcase. Really bad news.

"The witch who cursed your bloodline was named Smith."

"You could have told me that five minutes ago," I grumbled as I opened the S drawer. Not that it would help, with Smith being such a common name.

I flipped past sage, salt, and slime (ew). "Smith!" Flip, flip, flip. "Huh. There are only three, and they're all Isabel."

"That is her." Chaos's voice was full of menace.

I yanked the cards from the drawer and ducked between shelves as a fireball whizzed past. It smacked into a case of ancient-looking texts, but instead of setting the entire basement ablaze, it bounced off and returned to Ember's hand.

That was how fire magic was supposed to work.

Finding the books was easy-peasy, thanks to their librarian's organizational skills. I tugged them from the shelf and plopped onto the floor. The first one I opened was filled with healing spells, cleansing rituals, and other light magic stuff. I supposed even dark witches needed to lighten their loads from time to time. Playing with evil could take a toll.

"Isabel belonged to your coven before the curse."

That much I knew, but her name had been struck from the record books. Magically erased so she would never be spoken of again. "What turned her bad?"

"No rush, Ash. I'm having a blast." I couldn't tell if she said that with sarcasm or not. You never knew with Ember.

"I found the books," I called from the safety of the stacks.

"Let's take them all." Her sword met clay. The golem grunted.

"Then they'll know we've been here. They could locate them and cause us a mess of trouble." I flipped the pages.

"Good point." Slash, stab, grunt. "Continue."

"*A love triangle,*" Chaos answered. "*Isabel was betrothed to your great-great-great—*"

"Who knows how many greats? Got it."

"*Hester, your ancestor, arrived from England, and he fell in love with her, betraying Isabel.*"

"Oof. Hell hath no fury." The second book had tons of potions and spells of the unsavory variety, but nothing about the curse or where the skulls might be hidden. I put it back and opened the next one. "Bingo. This must be the one Cinder used to find Discord."

I ran my finger along the first page, a journal entry describing Isabel's pain and her intention. I only skimmed it, but let me just say... She was pissed.

The next page laid out the curse, how she did it, and the ramifications. Like Chaos said, she was supposed to pay with her soul.

Should my plan not work, their wrath will be exerted on my descendants. Return their skulls to them and beg for forgiveness, lest my entire lineage be doomed to hell.

CINDER CAME HERE ALONE. She had to find the book while fighting off the golem and get out undetected. How in Hell did she do it?

I flipped the page. "Good goddess, look at this." A map. A freaking map!

"Ugh!" Ember grunted before her head smacked the concrete floor at the end of the aisle. The golem dragged her out of my view.

"Shit! I'm coming, Em!" I ripped the map from the book, slammed it into its space on the shelf, and ran toward them. I skidded to a stop when I saw my sister dangling upside down from the creature's massive fist.

"Let her go!" I yanked the dagger from my thigh scabbard and hurled it at the golem. It hit him in the gut, but it disappeared inside him, his clay absorbing the weapon like a black hole. I grabbed a binding spell from my satchel, said the incantation, and threw it at him. Powder exploded in his face, and he dropped Ember—on her head—to wipe his eyes. He didn't freeze.

But my sister did.

The creature roared and started toward me. He swung his meaty arm, and I ducked. He clipped the top of my head, but my momentum carried me forward, and I slid toward Ember.

"Time to go." I hooked my arms beneath her shoulders and dragged her backward into the corridor.

"Use another spell." That Chaos. Ever helpful.

"If the binding spell didn't work, I doubt anything else will." I groaned and dragged her toward the stairs. It was all uphill from here. Literally.

"Let me help."

"How?" My foot met the first step as the golem prowled toward me. Yep, toying with the weaker one now that the threat was incapacitated. Demons were so predictable.

Chaos took my question as permission. My head spun, and I squeezed my eyes shut. When I opened them, the golem lay beneath one of seven toppled bookshelves. The library had been torn apart...in a state of complete...*chaos.*

"It won't hold him long. Run."

One foot behind the other, I got my sister up the stairs and through the meeting slash ritual room. I was about to drag her through the electrified door when Chaos yelled, "Stop!"

I froze. "What?"

"Her pendant is gone."

"Crappity crap. It must've fallen off when he held her upside down." I slipped mine off and put it around her neck along with my satchel.

"What's your plan?"

"Well, I have a whole other life inside me. A Prince of Hell. You can keep me safe, right? I doubt a little electricity would hurt you."

"I..."

"I'll let you take over like you did down there and in the kitchen. Get me through the spell and then give me back control." And then we'd have a long talk about consent.

"That's a horrible plan."

The sound of wood crashing echoed from below before feet pounded the stairs.

"Unless you have something better, do it now."

The golem roared, reached the top of the stairs, and lunged.

I blacked out, meaning Chaos took complete control. Yay. My plan worked.

Until it didn't. My demon got Ember through the spell no problem, but even without control of my body, I felt every magical jolt of electricity as it ripped through me, tearing my insides to shreds.

Then...nothing.

THIRTEEN

Every muscle in my body ached. My skin was raw, and the scent of burnt flesh assaulted my nose. I blinked my eyes open and squinted against the daylight streaming in through the windows. It felt like daggers through my pupils. I recoiled.

"There she is." Ember sat on the mattress next to me, and my blurry vision finally came into focus. To my right, a family photo taken in the library and a twelve-inch phoenix statue sat atop a wooden dresser. The closet door on the adjacent wall stood halfway ajar, and a stack of books lay on the nightstand next to me. We were in my bedroom.

"How the hell?" I tried to sit up, but my skin felt like it was tearing with every move I made. My head fell back on the pillow.

"Shh…" Ember gently touched my shoulder, sending pain slicing down my arm. "Don't move. Patrice is working on a spell to heal your burns."

"Burns?" How could I possibly have burns? I was a fire witch, and *that* part of my magic actually worked.

Ember nodded. "Electrical. How do you feel?"

"Extra crispy." The words rasped through my aching throat, and I winced.

"What were you thinking?" She brushed a strand of hair out of my face. "Why did you take your crystal off?"

"To put it on you. You lost yours in the fight." I cringed, the pinching motion of my face intensifying the pain.

"Here. Drink this. It'll help numb the pain until Patrice gets back." She held a straw to my lips, and I sipped the bitter liquid. Hints of amaranth, chamomile, and dandelion flooded my tastebuds.

"Can she pour it over your entire body? This pain is excruciating."

I laughed and winced again. "Hey, at least my plan worked."

Ember gave me another sip. "Chaos?"

I nodded. "He can't handle the pain."

"Typical man." She laughed. "Though he's probably the only reason we made it out."

"We wouldn't be in this pain if your plan had worked."

"We wouldn't be alive if it hadn't. How are we alive? How did we get here?"

Ember cut her gaze to the open door before getting up and closing it. "I told Patrice to let herself up when she had the potion." She lowered her voice. "After you froze me... Who knew magic wouldn't work on a golem, right?"

"Sorry about that."

She shrugged. "You didn't know. Anyway, after you froze me, and I realized no spells would work, I was sure we were done. But you, little sis, are stronger than you think. How did you get me up the stairs so quickly and away from the golem? Your spell wiped my memory for the time I was frozen."

"I dragged you. Chaos stalled the beast." The tea had eased the rawness in my throat a little. It did nothing for the rest of the pain.

"How?"

"I let him take over like he did in the kitchen. The golem went haywire and tore the library apart. While he was busy, I got you up the stairs. Then Chaos took over again to get us through the electricity spell. I blacked out after that."

"That makes sense. I can imagine the pain you must have felt, and if he felt it too... His power leaked out and gave me the biggest adrenaline spike I've ever felt. I busted through the freezing spell in time to watch the golem stop at the exit and fall back. He must be bound to the library. Anyway, I scooped you up and got the hell out."

"So much for getting in and out undetected. Do you think they'll retaliate?"

"Only if they figure out it was us. Tell me you know where the skulls are."

A knock sounded on the door before I could answer. "Everybody decent?" Patrice called from the other side.

Ember winked and pressed a finger to her lips in a *shh* gesture before opening the door. I could *shh* all she wanted. My throat felt like I'd swallowed the Sahara.

Sympathy crumpled Patrice's brow the moment her gaze locked on me. "Wow. You weren't kidding, Ember."

How bad did I look? I was tempted to ask for a mirror but thought better of it. I didn't want to know, and I certainly didn't want Chaos to see me looking like a blistered tomato. My status as the most beautiful witch he'd ever seen would be knocked down to zero.

Not that it mattered what he thought about my looks. It didn't, but he'd surely use my scorched skin as proof my plan didn't work, which it *did*.

Patrice swirled a bundle of straw in a mug and flicked the liquid over me. "How did you get electrical burns over your entire body?"

I looked at Ember, who luckily had already devised

a story that didn't involve us breaking laws and harboring a demon. "We had water in the basement. A breaker had flipped, so the power was out. Ash tried a spell to get the circuit running again, but it bounced off the reflective cover and hit the water. She was standing in it, and zap. She's lucky I heard the thud when she flew back onto the stairs."

Gee, thanks, Em. Way to make me look like an idiot.

"Only a fool would cast electricity while standing in water."

"No kidding." Whoops. No talking to Chaos in front of others. Why was that so hard to remember?

"This will make you feel so much better." Patrice finished sprinkling me with her potion. "Drink the rest of it." She offered me the mug.

I lifted my arm, and the searing pain of movement caused a garbled yelp to erupt from my throat. Ember took the container and pressed it to my lips, pouring it into my mouth slowly as I drank.

Patrice recited the incantation, and a glorious cooling sensation swept through my body, dulling the pain. The tension in my muscles eased, and I no longer felt like I'd been breaded and dropped into a vat of oil.

I lifted my arm. My skin felt like it was stretched too tightly over my frame, but I could move without sounding like an injured animal, so that was a plus. I pressed my fingertips to my cheek. Though the skin was smooth, it felt raw, like I'd stood on the windy beach too long in winter.

"Ahh. Sweet relief."

"You'll be tender for a bit." Patrice dropped the straw bundle into the mug and clutched it with both hands. "Take a cool bath tonight, and you'll be back to normal soon. No corsets until you are. They'll chafe."

"Thank you." I pushed to sitting, and my corset stayed on the bed where I'd lain.

Ember tossed me a t-shirt. "Sorry. Had to free the girls. You were burned beneath your clothes."

"Take care." Patrice flashed a sympathetic smile and slipped out the door.

I put on the shirt. The fabric felt like sandpaper against my skin. Could she not have picked something softer? "Do you have my bag?"

Ember gestured to the floor near the nightstand before tossing a pair of flannel pajama pants my way. I put them on and stood to look in the full-length mirror. Pink tinged my skin, but I was blister-free.

"The fabric rubbing your body is irritating. You should stay naked until you're healed."

"And look in every mirror I pass? You'd like that, wouldn't you?" I grabbed the satchel and set it on the bed before sinking onto the mattress.

"Very much."

Ember looked at me quizzically.

"Demons are perves." I grabbed the page I'd torn from the book.

"I merely suggested a way for us to heal faster."

"There is no 'us,' mister. This is my body, and you're about to vacate it." I peered at the map as Ember sat next to me. "It's not quite as detailed as I remember."

A lopsided pentagram took up most of the page while a few squiggly lines here and there could have indicated topography. A cross sat near the bottom right point of the star, and an arched line sat below the left side.

Ember pointed at a set of three wavy lines. "That could mean water. Do you think it's the ocean?"

"I don't know. There's water over here too." I pointed to the top left. "I bet the skulls are hidden at the points of the pentagram."

"Except there are five points and only three skulls. What's at the other two?"

"Traps."

I repeated Chaos's answer.

"Fabulous." Sarcasm laced my sister's voice.

"That's probably a church." I pointed at the cross. "If we can figure out which one, we can line it up with a modern map."

"This map is nearly four hundred years old. Whatever church it was, it's not there anymore."

"Good point. Most of the buildings from that time don't exist anymore."

"How did Cinder figure this out?" She took the paper and flipped it over. The back was blank. "What else did the book say?"

"Just a warning to her descendants that if her plan didn't work, they'd need to find the skulls and beg the demons for forgiveness."

She scoffed. "Like demons can forgive."

"If forgiveness is warranted, we can and do."

I couldn't tell you why Ember's assessment of demons irked me so much, but I snapped back, "They aren't all mindless monsters like the ones you've fought. They can be intelligent and even nice sometimes."

"I wouldn't go as far as nice."

Ember blinked twice before she replied. "I don't know what lines he's been feeding you, but he is a *demon*. A creature from Hell."

I narrowed my eyes. "A prince."

"Even worse."

My nostrils flared. "Chaos has done nothing but help us. If not for him, we'd still have no idea about the curse or what happened to Cinder."

She bristled. "If you'd read her journal first instead of tattooing yourself with a demonic sigil, we sure would."

"We'd still need him. We can't break the curse

without him." I crossed my arms and inclined my chin.

Ember laughed dryly. "You sound like you're glad you possessed yourself."

"Maybe I am. Getting to know him has opened my mind. Not all demons are bad."

"By your standards, yes, we are."

She shook her head. "I'm going to write this off as shock from your burns. Get your head straight and figure out this map. I'm going to work."

Ember turned on her heel and marched out the door, and I fought the urge to crumple the map in my hands. She didn't know Chaos like I did. Once I got him out of my head and into his physical form, she'd see.

"I think our bond is affecting you. I'm going to pull inward and go quiet for a while."

"Oh? You're not going to offer to destroy her like you did with Shade?"

"She's your blood. Family is sacred."

"Whatever." I slid the map into my satchel and carried it downstairs.

CHAPTER

FOURTEEN

A giant mug of coffee sat steaming on my desk as I scowled over the cryptic map. Ginger womaned the front of the shop today, so I had hours to focus until Ember came home. Plenty of time to figure this out, yet I couldn't concentrate.

After seeing the Boston coven's incredible library, I couldn't stand to look at mine. I wanted to fix it. To organize it and make it grand. But I had much more pressing matters to deal with.

I sipped my coffee and fired up my laptop. The public library had an entire room filled with books and articles on Salem's history. Sadly, none of it was digitized, so I'd have to take a trip to the town archives. Maybe getting away from my own would help me focus.

"You're frustrated." Chaos's voice startled me, and I nearly spilled my coffee on the map.

"That's a word for it." I set my mug aside and pressed my fingers to my temples. "I can't focus. The secrets are stacking up, and I'm horrible at keeping them. I feel bad for snapping at Ember... Why did I snap at her? I can't even remember what set me off."

"She made a generalization about my kind, and you felt it as an insult. You defended me."

I slid down in my chair and leaned my head back. "She doesn't know you."

"Neither do you. Have you forgotten why your sister and parents are missing? Why you're cursed? My brothers and I felt no remorse for making the deal with the witch Isabel. It's what we do."

He had a point. Whatever fondness I was beginning to feel for him, I needed to squash it like a cockroach. He was the reason for all this trouble. For everything. My forearm heated, and I pulled up my sleeve to see his sigil glowing red.

"It's our bond. As long as it exists, you'll feel a kinship with me, as I feel with you."

Well, that was good news. All I had to do was get him out of my head, and then I'd be able to think straight. Step one: go to the library and find a map of sixteen hundreds Salem.

"What's this?" Shade grabbed the map and

squinted at it. I'd been so caught up in my head, I hadn't heard him or Miles come in.

"Is that a map?" Miles peered over his shoulder. "That's the old church in Hingham, isn't it?" He pointed to the cross.

"How do you know that?" If only I could ask him for help. I jerked my sleeve down. "Is it still there?"

He shrugged. "I'm interested in cartography. Yeah, it's still there. It's the oldest in Massachusetts. Where did you get this?"

I yanked the map from Shade's hands and shoved it into my bag. "From a friend. It's a history project I'm working on. What do you want?"

"Ember didn't text you?" Shade picked up my coffee and took a sip. "This tastes like tar."

I ground my teeth and pulled out my phone. No messages, but that was no surprise. She was pissed at me, as she should have been. I was out of line defending a demon. "What do you want?" I asked again.

"Wow." He set my mug down and clicked his tongue. "The sister of the acting High Priestess doesn't even know what's going on. How sad."

"My offer with him still stands."

I fought a grin. If only.

"We need sigils," Miles said. "We've located a small rift in the veil, and a couple of gnomes got through. They're digging up someone's garden."

I snorted. "Gnomes? Why do you need sigils for gnomes? They're two feet tall."

Shade squared his shoulders at me, fisting his hands to make his muscles flex. "They're also hungry and venomous. Are you going to do your job, or should I contact the Higher Power and ask them to send us a real Ink Master?"

Chaos's growl reverberated through my entire body, but if it was audible, the guys didn't react. I straightened my spine, staring at Shade as I chose my words. The string of profanities I wanted to throw at him would only drag me down to his level.

"This is ridiculous." Shade's nostrils flared, and a wildness filled his eyes. "I can't believe someone like you has such a high rank in the coven." He swiped his arm across my desk, sending my coffee, lamp, and laptop crashing to the floor. As he stomped toward the closest bookcase, he jabbed his fingers into his hair and pulled at the roots.

"This setup is shit." He knocked over a stack of books and kicked one across the room. "This coven doesn't work." He grabbed the bookcase and rocked it, trying to pull it down. It was too big, weighted more heavily at the bottom so it stayed upright.

"Ahhrrgh!" He went for the books, grabbing them two at a time and hurling them to the floor. He'd gone crazy. He was acting like total...

"Chaos..." I said through clenched teeth.

He growled in answer.

"Stop it right now," I said to both the demon in my head and the man tearing apart my library. Neither obeyed.

I shot to my feet and screamed, "I said stop!"

Chaos grunted, and Shade froze, looking at the mess he'd made with confusion in his eyes.

"Are you finished with your temper tantrum?" Again, I spoke to them both.

"I..." Shade looked at his hands, his eyes widening as his gaze locked on my laptop covered in coffee.

"He deserved worse."

I pressed my lips into a hard line. Chaos would get a reaming later, for sure. Right now, I needed to get these guys set and out of my building.

"Is everything okay?" Ginger stood in the doorway, alarm tightening her features. "What happened?"

Chaos happened, but I couldn't let them know that. "Shade threw a hissy fit when his words didn't cut me deep enough."

He looked at his hands again. "I didn't. I don't..."

"The evidence suggests otherwise." I put my things back on my desk and threw a stack of napkins onto the puddle of coffee.

"Are you okay?" Miles asked him, and he nodded. Of course Shade's new little pet would only be concerned about his owner and not about the disaster he just caused.

"Come on." I brushed past them. "Let's get those sigils done before the gnomes eat all the cats in Salem."

They followed me into the studio, and Ginger returned to the front of the shop. I put on my professional face and gifted the boys with thicker skin and resistance to venom. As I put the finishing touch on Miles's tattoo, my sleeve slipped up, revealing a bit of Chaos's symbol.

"What do you need a sigil for?" he asked.

I yanked my sleeve down and returned the tattoo machine to its stand. "Protection from bullshit." I cut my gaze over to Shade, who still looked confused as hell. I knew the feeling.

Did he apologize for the mess he made? No. Did I expect him to? Not really, but it would've been nice. At any rate, he owed me a new laptop if the one he knocked off the desk was broken. Actually, Chaos owed me a new laptop.

"Thanks for your help," Miles said. "Sorry about the mess."

"Yeah. Thanks," Shade muttered before shuffling out the door.

"Have fun fighting gnomes," I called as they walked away.

With the guys out of my hair, I returned to the

library to grab my bag. My jaw tightened at the disorder, but I would have to deal with it later. I locked up the stacks and the entrance to our apartment and slipped out the back door.

Brisk wind stung my still tender cheeks, and as I hung a right on Essex Street, I pressed my phone to my ear so I could gripe out Chaos without looking like a total whack job. "What the hell was that? I told you not to mess with him."

"He disrespected you."

"Shade always disrespects me. It's nothing new."

"He needs to learn his place."

I rolled my eyes. "He knows his place. That's why he acts the way he does. I bruised his fragile ego."

"And he is determined to bruise yours."

We passed a witchy shop and a monster museum. Dozens of tourists milled about, looking into store windows and chatting. The sun shone high in a cloudless sky, its heat helping tame the bitter wind.

"You can't go around making people crazy, especially when I have explicitly told you to leave someone alone." I stopped in front of a resale shop and sighed. Who knew what magical artifacts or books occupied the shelves in there, and it was my job to root them out. Yet another task that kept moving farther down on my to-do list.

"I won't allow anyone to harm you."

"He's not harming me." I continued on my way to

the town archives. "I'd tell you to get it through your thick skull, but since you don't have one at the moment..."

"*Funny.*"

"Seriously, though. Don't do that again."

"*I make no promises.*"

"Of course you don't. You're a demon."

"*Exactly.*"

My face pinched, no doubt making me look like a sour kangaroo, but whatever. I had two annoying men battling for my last nerve and a daunting quest that seemed damn near impossible to complete. A nap and a stiff drink would do me good, but I didn't have time for either.

A sense of calm washed over me as I approached the three-story brown brick building. I ascended the stone steps toward the entrance, a set of wooden double doors with columns on both sides holding up a small portico, and rested my hand against the textured concrete pillar.

"No matter what we find, who we see, or what happens in here, you are not, under any circumstances, to take over and make me or anyone else tear this place apart."

"*Again, I make no promises.*"

Not good enough. I curled my hand into a fist. "I mean it, Chaos. Libraries are sacred spaces that deserve our respect. They're the only public buildings you can go to and just be. No one expects you to buy anything. You don't have to have a reason to be there. I need you to promise me you won't cause trouble in here. You've damaged enough libraries."

He grunted. *"I won't apologize for stopping the golem from killing you, but I do regret making Shade damage your belongings."*

"Promise me."

A mother and her small daughter exited the building, the girl's arms full of picture books, a smile brightening her face. The mom looked at me quizzically as she passed. Crap. I'd absently returned the phone to my pocket, so I looked like I was talking to myself.

"Chaos…" I fished my earbuds from my bag and put one in before tucking my hair behind my ear so it would show.

Silence for one beat. Two. *"I promise I will try."*

That would have to suffice. "Okay. Let's do this." I stepped over the threshold and took a deep breath. Ahhh… Books.

A curved staircase led up to the third floor, and I had to force myself not to climb it two steps at a time. On the top floor, the city archives room stood in the back of the building. I passed row after row of reference books, all shelved in their proper places, and a smile tugged at the corners of my mouth.

"You enjoy this place?"

"I'm a librarian," I whispered. "Of course I do." Especially the reference section. Books were my jam.

Lucky for me, no one else needed to look up Salem's history today. I had the room to myself. Dropping my bag on the table, I strode to the computer kiosk on the far wall. At least their card catalog went digital. A quick search pointed me to a volume detailing the layout of sixteen hundreds Salem and the surrounding area.

"See how easy it is to locate things when they're organized?" I found the book on the third shelf, right where it was supposed to be, and set it on the table.

"Some thrive in chaotic environments."

I opened it to the table of contents. "Do they really, though? I mean, you're a demon called 'Chaos,' and your brothers are 'Discord' and 'Mayhem.' Are there any princes of Hell called 'Order' or 'Organization?' If so, I don't see how they could possibly be scary."

"Not all demons are meant to instill fear. Some gain trust before unleashing their wrath."

"Uh-huh. But are there any demons whose power is organization?"

"No."

"That's what I thought." The table of contents wasn't nearly detailed enough for a five-inch-thick book, so I flipped to the index to find the right page. "Here we go. The oldest map of Salem."

I tugged the pentagram map from my bag to

compare the two. Sure enough, the squiggly lines did indicate water, which helped me line it up. The cross was the church Miles thought it was. Damn. If I could get him away from Shade for long enough, he might be able to help figure out exactly where the points on the pentagram indicated. I doubted these were drawn to precise scale considering their age.

I snapped a picture of the map with my phone. I'd have to blow it up to make it the same size as Isabel's. As I shoved my phone into my pocket, the energy in the room shifted and Chaos growled.

"Do you sense it?"

I focused on the sensation, a faint disturbance in the vibration, so low I would have never detected it if Chaos hadn't taught me what to look for.

"Demon," I whispered and snapped my head from side to side. The room appeared empty, but there was no mistaking the low vibration in my bones. "Where?"

"Another rift has opened. It senses me."

"A rift *inside* the library?" Oh no. I could not allow a demon to wreak havoc on this archive. I grabbed a bottled perimeter location spell, closed the door for privacy, and blew the dust into the air.

The cloud billowed, collecting around a teeny tiny tear in the veil, no bigger than the palm of my hand. I could seal that before the beastie even made it through. Uncorking the bottle of veil-mending magic, I prepared to toss it on the opening, but a set of spindly fingers with suction cups on the ends like a frog grabbed the sides of the tear and ripped it open.

A one-foot-tall troll-looking creature hopped through, sneered at me, and headed straight for the marble bust of the city's founder, Roger Conant, standing on a dais in the corner. It climbed the statue, bared its pointy teeth, and bit into old Conant's head.

"What the hell is that?"

"*An imp. A low-level demon incapable of speech or rational thought.*"

"Great." I set the veil healing spell on the table. "How do I vanquish it?"

"*Pierce its heart. Only one, in the center of its chest.*"

The imp gnawed on the statue, making an *om nom nom* sound until one of its teeth snapped. It hissed at the bust, its hand covering its mouth as it darted to the floor and backed away. Its nostrils flared, and it crawled across the tile, using its long arms to propel it like a monkey.

"That would be easy-peasy if I had a weapon on me." I moved around the table, putting distance between the little monster and myself.

The imp reached for a book on the bottom shelf, and I shouted, "Hey! Hands off."

It hissed and grabbed the volume, anyway. Then it took a giant bite out of the spine.

"Son of a serpent. That is not the way to devour a

book. Drop it." I clapped and stomped my feet, trying to scare it. I was rewarded with another hiss.

"Perhaps a freezing spell?"

"You think?" I grabbed the potion from my bag, which would now have to be restocked *again*, and threw it on the little fiend while I recited the incantation. The half-eaten book dropped to the floor, and the imp froze with an *oh shit* expression on its hideous face.

Okay, now what? I had nothing to stab it with. "Can I shove it back through like we did the faeries?"

I didn't wait for an answer. Gripping it by the slimy shoulders, I hoisted it from the ground and pushed it into the rift. It wouldn't pass through. I shoved again, really putting my weight into it, but all I managed to do was get imp slime all over my shirt.

"What am I doing wrong?" I set it on the floor. That little guy was heavier than he looked.

"The imp wasn't summoned from Hell. He escaped, drawn to my energy. As long as I'm here, he can't be forced through."

"But the faeries could?" I wiped my hands on my pants.

"They aren't demons."

"Great, and as long as I'm here, you're here. But if I leave, he'll eat the rest of the books."

"The only option is to vanquish him."

"Which requires a weapon." I scanned the shelves. "I could knock him on the head with a big book."

"You must pierce his heart."

"Fabulous." If only I wore stilettos, I could stomp him like a grape and make him go splat. I blew out a hard breath. The door rattled, someone trying to come in.

"Huh," a voice sounded from outside. "It's locked. Let me get the key. Be right back."

"Well, crap." Someone wanted in the archives, and a visible rift floated in the air while a demon lay on the floor. I had about two minutes to clean up this mess before all hell broke loose.

Well, technically, I guess a little hell had already broken loose.

I spun in a circle, taking in the room. Books, books, more books, computer kiosk, more books. Crap on a cracker. Nothing even remotely close to a weapon called this space home. I wrung my hands, my mind scrambling to come up with a plan.

"A little help, Chaos?"

"I can stall the people outside by—"

"No. No, you can't." I wrung my hands again, and a jagged fingernail scratched my palm. I was way overdue for a manicure, but that was so far down my list it had fallen off the bottom.

The imp let out a muffled screech, its arm

twitching as the spell began losing its hold. I chewed on my broken nail. I was screwed.

Wait... I looked at my finger and sucked in a breath. Of course! I had a metal nail file in my bag. I rummaged through and found my mini manicure set. I grabbed the file and held it up. "Do you think this will work?"

"I think it's our only shot."

The imp's lips peeled back over its tiny fangs, and it hissed as I approached. I couldn't think about what I was doing, or I'd talk myself out of it, so I gritted my teeth and jabbed the file into the slimy creature's chest.

It wailed once, turned into a puff of smoke, and the rift sucked it back through. Whew.

"Here we go," the librarian's voice came from right outside the door.

"Not yet," I whispered and darted toward it. I still had to seal the rift and clean up the mess.

Holding my hands over the lock, I whispered another incantation I'd used frequently growing up— a locking spell. That should hold them. I wasn't sure why I didn't think of doing that earlier. I would blame it on stress. The door rattled, the knob turning back and forth, but it wouldn't budge.

I allowed myself one deep breath before I sealed the rift. Fatigue made my head spin, and I stumbled as I returned the half-eaten book to the shelf. Hopefully it wasn't the only copy available. I reshelved the volume I'd been reading and gathered my things before releasing the lock.

Swinging the door inward, I gasped, pretending to be startled by the people across the threshold. "Oh, excuse me." I tried to shuffle past them.

"This door is supposed to remain open," the librarian scolded.

"Sorry. Someone was on their phone out there, and it was distracting. I won't do it again." I hurried to the staircase and darted down the steps, hoping they didn't notice the imp slime covering my shirt.

I made it outside without any more issues, and I stopped by a tree a block away. My pulse thrummed, and it took a minute to catch my breath, but it was done. "Well, that was fun."

"Indeed. You handled that like the powerful witch you are. I'm impressed."

"Please." I strode across the intersection and headed home. "I vanquished him with a nail file. I'd hardly call that the actions of a powerful witch."

"You improvised, and you prevailed."

"I am good at that, apparently." Two more blocks, and I could peel these slimy clothes off. Yuck. "You said the imp sensed you, and that's why the rift formed? How does that work?"

"The veil was already thin in the library. The imp was drawn to my energy when we stepped inside, and it

was able to tear the veil as it was compelled to be near me."

Fabulous. Lower-level creatures could already slip through thin spots without any help. "Can't you turn your bat signal off while we take care of this? I don't need imps breaking through everywhere I go."

"If had had a corporeal form, I would have more control. With you as my host, I'm afraid my energy bleeds through your skin, creating a beacon for all demons."

"Great. So the rifts are going to follow us wherever we go?"

"And it will only get worse. Our bond is solidifying faster than I thought it would. My power permeates your form, and your human flesh can't hold it in."

"Wait." I stopped in my tracks and pressed my hand to my chest. "What are you saying? I thought we had two weeks before you took over completely. You said I was the order to your madness."

"At the rate we're bonding, it's more like two days."

"We're not bonding any faster than we were before. What changed since yesterday?" A pendant in the thrift shop window caught my gaze, and I stopped to look at it. An upside-down pentagram embossed on what looked like bone hung from a black cord.

"You allowed me to control your form twice."

"So? What makes you think that sped things along?"

"You lashed out at your sister for making a generaliza-

tion about my kind. You're growing fond of me."

I laughed dryly. "Believe me, buddy, I am not growing fond of you. Getting you out of my head is my number one priority." Right after I checked this arti- fact for magic. I glanced left and right to be sure no one was watching before I whispered my magic- revealing spell.

"Really? Because I'm growing fond of you. Before you summoned me, I would rather have plucked my eyes out with a pitchfork than have relations with a witch."

My gold sparkles passed through the glass, hovered over the items in the window, and then dissi- pated. No magic, thank the goddess.

"You've been in a dark prison for hundreds of years. You're fond of anything with boobs." I turned away from the window and froze. A group of people on a history tour formed a circle around a man with a wild look in his eyes. He jabbed his fingers into his hair and ran toward another man in the group.

His target didn't move. The man bounced off his chest and careened into a woman. She shoved him, and all hell broke loose. They shouted and pushed each other, grabbed each other's bags, and dumped the contents on the ground. It was total...

Yep, you guessed it. Chaos.

"We need to get inside."

"No kidding." I turned on my heel and booked it the last block to our building.

CHAPTER

FIFTEEN

"Two days?" Ember shouted through the phone. "Why didn't you call me sooner?"

"I literally just found out. I called you as soon as I washed the imp slime off and changed clothes." I set an enchanted crystal in the corner of my bedroom and activated the ward.

"Where are you?"

"In my bedroom. I set up a shield to hold in magic, so he won't bleed out past my door." I'd also sent Ginger home and locked up the shop. With all the magic I'd used in a short amount of time, to say I was spent was an understatement.

"Stay there. I'm coming home." She ended the call, and I dropped onto the bed, exhausted.

The second my lids closed, an image of the man with dark hair and green eyes played through my mind. He stood six-foot-four and had a broad, muscular chest and abs I could do laundry on. Fire flashed in his eyes as he prowled toward me, and his low vibration wrapped around me, sinking all the way to my bones.

Whether I was dreaming or not, a normal person would have shit their pants if a big, predatory Prince of Hell looked at them like he wanted to consume them. Not me. Every nerve in my body tingled, and I smiled.

He inhaled deeply, his brows drawing down like he wasn't sure if he should devour me in a fun way or a literal way. My pulse thrummed, and I rested my hands against the smooth skin on his chest. Heat permeated my fingertips to pool in my core.

"Ash, wake up." Ember poked my shoulder, drawing me from my dream. "I gave you an hour to recharge, but we've got to get moving."

I sat up and rubbed my arms as if I could chase away the sensation of my hormones flaring to life over a demon. My mind sure had fabricated a sexy one. *Oof.*

"Mmm... Another good dream?" Chaos teased.

I ignored him. "Sorry. Too much spellwork." I swung my legs over the side of the bed and grabbed my boots.

"Tell me about the imp. What happened? Did you find a map? Why did you set up a ward?" She paced at the foot of my bed, her hands curling into fists before splaying and curling again.

I laced up my boots. "I'm sorry for snapping at you earlier. It's the bond. As soon as I get him out of my head, I'll be normal again."

"I figured as much." She stopped pacing and rested a hand on her hip. "What happened?"

I relayed the events in the library, vanquishing the imp, and the effect I...Chaos...had on the tourists. "So I set up the ward to keep his magic contained while I rested."

"Your fatigue weakened my ability to keep my magic in check. I'm better now."

She arched a brow. "A nail file?"

"It was all I had."

"Not bad, little sis." She nodded her approval. "Did you find a map?"

I showed her the photo. "When Miles came in for a sigil, he recognized the cross as the old church in Hingham. He says it's still there." I pulled Isabel's map out of my bag. "He studies cartography. If he wasn't so far up Shade's ass, I'd suggest we pick his brain for the other locations."

"Absolutely not. We will handle this on our own." Ember laid the paper map on my mattress and compared the image on my phone. "We need to print this." She tapped the screen a few times, and the printer hummed to life down the hall. She handed me the phone and strode out of the room.

"Any guess as to where your skull might be?" I peered at the pentagram. "Did she give you any clues when she vanquished you?"

"None. She imprisoned us before she hid our skulls."

"Fabulous. I wonder, though." I grabbed my crystal pendulum and held it over the map. The metal chain felt cool in my grip, and as I swung it in circles over the pentagram, I focused my intent on finding Chaos's skull.

My chest heated, my magic humming to life. I stilled my hand, letting the crystal's momentum guide it to one of the points on the star. The motion slowed until the pendulum hung still, right in the middle of the map.

"Well, that sucks. I was hoping a little divination would show us where to go." I returned the pendulum to the shelf.

"Isabel would not make our skulls so easy to find."

I shrugged. "It was worth a shot."

Ember returned with a printed version of the pic I snapped."We know for sure this is the church?" She angled the printout so the two maps lined up.

"It looks that way. See the water here and here?" I pointed to Isabel's squiggly lines and then at the library's map.

"And these other points? What are they? Did Miles say anything else?"

"I don't know. I snatched it out of Shade's hands before they could examine it more closely. We'll have to go to each point and see if Chaos can sense anything."

"I'm certain she hid them behind a spell. Your magic-revealing incantation will help before I could possibly sense anything...unless she has demons guarding the locations."

"Ugh. Please, no more golems." I pointed to the church on the map. "I say we start there. At least we know exactly what place we're looking for."

Ember nodded. "Agreed. Let's go."

"I need to restock my kit. Give me twenty minutes." I followed her out of my room.

"You also need food. Keeping up your strength will help you keep me in check."

"I'll grab a few energy bars, and then I'll have no problem putting you in a time-out."

He did that growly purr again, and I shivered in a good way. Yeah, this bond needed to be broken ASAP.

After I threw together a few premade spells and stocked my kit, we climbed into the van and headed to Hingham. It took an hour by car, so I could only imagine what the trek must've been like way back when. Did Isabel walk? Go on horseback? Arrive by boat? A woman scorned and cursed to spend eternity in Hell was capable of anything, I supposed.

"She did not want these skulls found, did she?" Ember hung a left on Main Street and rolled to a stop in front of the church. "Why so far away?"

"She and her entire bloodline are cursed. I bet she'd have gone farther if she had the means." I slid out of the van and slipped my satchel onto my shoulder. The church was a two-story beige wooden structure with a steeple. It sat atop a little hill, and a black fence surrounded it.

"Does Chaos sense anything demonic?" Ember asked as she strode toward the front door.

"Nothing, but it will be masked by magic."

"He doesn't. Let me check the area for spells before we barge inside. She probably hid the skull in a crypt or basement. That's what I would do."

I stood at the gate and recited my favorite incantation, casting my magic wide to cover most of the front lawn. Gold sparkled in the air and dissipated as it fell to the ground. "Nothing out here."

I moved closer and cast the spell on the building. I expected to see at least a little magic around the doorway, but the glitter dissolved like it had on the lawn. The sun sank into the horizon, turning the sky shades of purple and red, and an early-riser owl hooted from the tree to our right.

"Inside or around back?" Ember asked.

"Back." I turned and headed around the building. I couldn't say why I felt drawn that way, but I did.

Maybe it was a hunch. Maybe I'd cast my spell so many times I didn't need it anymore. Who knew?

As we rounded the back of the building, I headed straight for the cellar door. The energy here felt different. Like it used to spark with magic, but it had now gone stale. "Am I sensing demonic energy?"

Ember drew her sword. "I don't know. Are you?"

"I sense nothing."

"No. It must be something else." I heaved the door open and descended the steps, still feeling drawn to something by who knew what.

The basement looked typical of old homes that were built before electricity and indoor plumbing became the norm. Metal tubing ran along the walls, enclosing the wiring that had been added later, and exposed ductwork stretched across the ceiling. Some shelves stood against the far wall, but I wasn't interested in those. A staircase next to them led up to the ground floor, but I hung a left, the stale magic sensation pulling me to a waist-high door with a broken padlock.

I started to tug the door open, but I paused, letting the energy wash over me. I didn't feel the low vibration in my bones, but I waited for Chaos to chime in before I continued. "Anything?" I asked him.

"There is no demonic energy in this basement, but I sense a rift forming outside. Another lower-level demon has sensed my magic."

"Crap. Okay. Em?"

"Yeah?" She turned from the bookcase she'd been examining.

"I've got this. Can you head up and vanquish the demon that's about to crossover?"

She grinned. "With pleasure."

Ember bounded up the stairs, and I opened the small door. A tunnel stretched out before me, the stale magic culminating at the end. I crawled inside. Crazy, I know. I was usually much more cautious, but somehow I *knew* whatever hex was used to seal this corridor had been broken.

I reached the end and cast my spell. Glitter clung to the walls, revealing the smoky cloaking spell that used to hide this space. No active magic remained. "There was a skull here."

Chaos growled. *"Discord. I sense his energy."*

"Look at this," I said, as if he had a choice. He saw everything I saw, including the two-foot wooden cube sitting in the back corner. Its hinged lid stood open, revealing emptiness inside. "You're right. It was sealed with magic."

"My brother's skull was in there."

"Well, it's gone now."

"Obviously."

I shined my phone's flashlight around the space and gasped. There, pinned to the dirt wall with an array of daggers, hung the rotting corpse of a five-foot-long hairless dog. Broken capillaries created a reddish web over its ashy skin, and its yellow eyes bulged from their sockets. Curling my lip, I backed out of the tunnel and dusted off my pants.

"Cinder found this place, broke the spell, and killed the beastie guarding it."

"She defeated a hellhound. Your sister is powerful."

"No kidding."

"It runs in the family."

"Most of the time." I swept the basement to be sure we didn't leave any signs of magic behind before heading up the steps. The evening had bled into full dark by the time I reached the surface, and I looked across the yard in time to see my sister do her famous spin and swing, lopping off the head of the demon who'd crawled through the rift.

One of its horns stuck in the dirt, keeping it from rolling down the hill, and as she reached down to grab it, the whole thing crumbled to ash before getting sucked through the tear in reality.

"Why could that one be killed by beheading, but the others had to be stabbed through the heart?" I strode toward the rift, searching my bag for the sealing spell along the way.

"Because that kind has no heart. It was an immature incubus."

"Yikes." I found the right bottled spell, and Ember and I joined forces to seal the rift. It was bigger than the last one, and we all saw what happened when I got too tired and Chaos bled out. Well, Ember didn't see, but I'd given her a pretty good description.

She wiped her sword with a handkerchief and slid it into her back scabbard. "What did you find in there?"

I jerked my head toward the van. We'd gotten lucky so far, and no one had shown up to question us. Best not to press it. "Cinder was there. It's where she found Discord's skull."

She started toward the parking lot. "Are you sure?"

I nodded. "Chaos sensed his brother's energy, and I sensed..." What did I sense? I was still trying to wrap my mind around it. "I recognized her handiwork." I climbed into the van.

Ember stowed her weapons before getting into the driver's seat and starting the engine. "How are you feeling? Do you have it in you to hit another one tonight?"

"I don't have a choice, do I? There are four more possible hidey-holes, and I have about thirty-six hours left to live."

"We must find my skull before then."

"That's the plan." I laid the maps on my lap. "How do we want to tackle this? Go clockwise and hit them all in order?"

"Works for me." Ember located the general area on

the GPS and pulled up the directions. "It's an hour away too. Counter-clockwise would be faster."

I was about to agree with her when a nagging sensation pulled in my gut. "Hold on. We know Discord's skull was here. Would she really hide another in the next closest spot?"

"You think she did every other point on the star?"

"And set traps at the other two." I tapped the map.

"You're overthinking this. If she skipped the next point clockwise, the last skull would still be located at the point next to Discord's."

"You're right. That doesn't make sense." I chewed my lower lip. Overthinking was my specialty.

Ember pulled to the side of the road. "Tell me where we're going."

"You felt a pull in your gut. That is your magic speaking to you. Listen."

I laughed. "My magic doesn't work like that."

"Most of your magic is yet untapped. You found the hiding place in the church without a spell. Trust yourself."

"I used spells." I rolled my eyes. "He's telling me to trust my gut because I kinda knew where the first skull was hidden. But I used spells to confirm it. I could have just as easily been wrong."

Ember arched a brow. "But you were right."

I shrugged one shoulder.

She screwed her mouth to one side like she wasn't sure she wanted to say what she was about to say.

"Dad can do that, you know. It's why the mess in the library never bothered him."

I shook my head. "He used location spells to find things."

She grabbed my hand, stilling my drumming fingers. "He taught *you* the location spell to find things. He just *knew* where to look, and he was trying to help you realize that magic in yourself. It's a rare power, Ash, and he was sure you had it. I'm sure too."

Wait. What? *That* was why he kept the library in a shambles? He was naturally drawn to whatever he needed to find, so the mess didn't matter to him. It mattered to me, though. It drove...it still drives...me crazy, but there was a method to his madness.

I gazed at the map, and tears gathered on my lower lids. All this time, I thought my dad was wasting his energy casting location spells to find books that could be easily organized, when he could simply sense them with his inborn power. Could he have been trying to bring out the same power in me? Could I...?

I swallowed the thickness from my throat. "We don't know that I inherited it."

Ember squeezed my hand, and I sniffled. If he had just told me what was going on, our relationship would have been so much smoother.

"I got into so many arguments with him over the mess. Why didn't he tell me what he was doing?"

"Honestly?" She released my hand and gripped the

steering wheel. "Your self-esteem was already so low because your fire magic isn't as prevalent as mine and Cinder's. If he told you he wanted you to develop another power, and you couldn't, you might've never recovered."

I laughed dryly and wiped my tears. That sounded about right. "Well, if I have that power—and I'm not saying I do—I have no idea how I tapped into it at the church. And dad's not here to guide me."

"I can guide you."

"You're a demon. Why do you think you can guide me?"

"Because I feel the power too. The tugging in your gut is your magic speaking to you. I can help you listen."

Great. The parasite inside me was more familiar with my magic than I was. Figured. "Why the hell not? I'll be dead in a day otherwise, so what have I got to lose?"

Ember grinned. "That's the spirit, sis."

I stared at the map, willing the gut tug to take hold, but nothing happened. I breathed deeply, relaxing my muscles and letting my vision blur. No tug.

Another deep breath. I rolled my neck, loosening the tension and allowing the energy around me to guide my thoughts.

Nothing happened.

Of course nothing happened. I knew it wouldn't. "Well, what now?" I asked no one in particular.

"Give it time to build. Clear your mind of everything but the map."

"Right. Sure." With my elbow on the armrest, I pressed my fingers to my temple. "Let me not think about my impending death that's looming closer by the second."

Ember clasped my shoulder. "You can do this."

I nodded and stared at the map again. "I can do this." My life depended on it.

"Focus."

I fixed my gaze on the pentagram, letting everything around it go fuzzy. Cinder was counting on me. Mom and Dad could still be saved. Maybe.

"Focus..." Chaos reminded me. *"There. Do you feel it?"*

The fact he felt it before me was a bad sign in the *how much time does Ash have left before a demon takes over her body?* department, but yeah. I felt it. I sensed a gentle tugging in my stomach, trying to tell me where to look.

"Think specifically about my skull. Mayhem's can wait."

Four possible destinations and only one of them could save my life. "It makes sense to go to the closest one."

"You won't find it by logic. Use your gift."

He was right. I knew he was right, but my brain was battling for control. I always used logic. Wasn't that my gift? Thinking rationally. Keeping things in order. Planning. Organizing.

"Ash..."

Grrr... I had to let go of my thoughts. Which one felt right?

My muscles tensed, my nails digging into my palms as I squeezed my fists. My first thought was clockwise. But counterclockwise would get us to a destination faster. Or maybe we should try the top point.

"What is your gut telling you?"

Without another thought, I dropped my finger onto the map. "Counterclockwise."

"Are you sure?" Ember asked.

"Yes." It was the closest point. It made sense to go there next.

She nodded once and put the van in gear. "Here we go."

Chaos stayed silent. Whether he agreed with my choice or not, he didn't say. I took the quiet as an opportunity to recharge my vim and leaned my head against the window. The glass felt cold against my skin, and the gentle vibration of the wheels on the road lulled me to sleep.

I woke as Ember shut off the engine in a mall parking lot. The good news: it had closed at eight p.m.

Few cars dotted the lot, which meant the employees closing shop were the only ones inside.

The bad news: shopping malls didn't exist in the sixteen hundreds, so finding the next hidey hole would be impossible.

I straightened in my seat and compared the two maps. "Are we sure this is the place?"

Ember turned her hand palms up. "No. I drove around to see if an old building still stood, but this town is as modern as can be. Whatever structure she hid it in is long gone now. Maybe you can sense it."

My cheeks puffed as I blew out a breath. "I can try."

Ember holstered her weapons, and I grabbed my satchel before we crept through the parking lot toward the mall entrance. Lights attached to towering poles cast circles of illumination on the asphalt, and a paper fast food bag tumbled by in the wind.

A man wearing jeans and a red flannel exited the mall, snapping his gaze in our direction. Ember yanked me down behind a pickup truck. "Do we have any more of Shade's spells?"

I checked the bag and did not curl my lip in disgust. Yay me. "One. Should I activate it?"

"I can't walk around with all these weapons without garnering unwanted attention, so yeah. We don't have a choice."

I uncorked the bottle and activated the spell,

cloaking us in a shadow that would follow for at least five minutes. Ten if we were lucky. Ember straightened, and I followed her toward the entrance. She goosed the man in the side as we passed, and he squealed, rubbing his ribs like something bit him before darting to the Mazda in the back of the lot. My sister snickered. I rolled my eyes.

"Ember likes to antagonize."

"You should've seen her when we were kids." I stopped in front of the left side door while Ember tried them all, beginning at the right.

"They're locked," she said. "Got your picking kit?"

I reached for the handle in front of me and tugged the door open, gesturing for her to enter.

"See?" She strode inside. "You do have dad's power. You knew exactly which door was unlocked."

"I paid attention to which one the guy left through." I followed her in and tugged the door shut behind me.

"Attention to detail is a powerful tool too." She rested a hand on her hip. "Where to now?"

"I feel the tug. Do you? It's behind your navel."

I focused on the sensation in my belly, and sure enough, it was there, just like at the church. I couldn't see the location in my mind, but an invisible force guided me down the corridor. The path split, and I followed it to the right without hesitation. A single door, painted beige to match the wall, stood between a shoe store and a candy factory.

"This way." I motioned for Ember to follow and stepped through the door.

She lit a fireball to light the darkened hallway, and we made our way down, taking a sharp left turn at the end before descending a steep staircase into the basement. The massive furnace and metal ductwork gave off Freddy Krueger vibes, but my target was a piece of plywood nailed to the wall and blocked with an empty shelving unit.

"Help me move this." I grabbed one side, my sister got the other, and a screech pierced my eardrums as we dragged it across the floor.

I scanned the area for a crowbar or anything we could use to pry the wood from the wall. Ember had her own idea. She slammed her boot into the wood, knocking a jagged hole in the center. She kicked again and one more time before grabbing the splintered pieces and tearing them out, making a hole big enough for us to pass through.

"You should have let me check it for magic before you busted it down," I said.

"Oops." She gestured to the opening, and I cast my spell, sending golden sparkles on the hunt for magic.

A few stuck, revealing a faint disturbance in the air, like a magical heatwave. "It's old, but there's a ward here. Not on the wood; it was cast long before the space was covered."

Ember nodded. "Give people the heebie jeebies so they won't want to continue into the tunnel."

"It must've worked. They sealed it off."

Ember climbed into the forbidden space, and I followed. The deeper in we went, the more unfinished the space became. The wood floor gave way to dirt, the walls going from studs and support beams to plain old earth.

The tunnel stretched on for another fifty yards before spilling out into a small chamber about the size of my bedroom. A sickening feeling joined the pull in my gut, and I grabbed Ember's arm, stopping her from entering the room.

"What?" she asked.

"Something doesn't feel right." My head spun, my vision wavering. "Chaos? Are you picking up anything?"

Silence answered me.

"Now is not the time for you to go dormant, mister. Help me interpret these feelings." A wave of nausea washed over me, and I tightened my grip on Ember's arm. "I don't feel good."

My sister took both my hands in hers. "We're so close. Help me cast the magic-revealing spell, and you can sit out the rest of this adventure."

"This is bad, Em. I don't know what's happening."

My vision tunneled, glowing red around the edges. "I can't..."

"C'mon, sis. I can't do it without the potion, so unless you've got one ready-made in that bag of yours..."

"Confess, expose..." I shook my head, and the room tilted.

"You've got this." Ember's power flowed into me, bringing everything back into focus.

"Confess, expose my magic sleuth. I call on you to reveal your truth." My knees buckled, and Ember helped me to the ground.

"I'm sorry. I held back as long as I could." My mouth formed the words. They filled the room with my voice. But I wasn't the one talking.

"*Chaos?*" I asked, but my mouth didn't work.

"We don't have much time." My body rose, a newfound strength running through my limbs, yet I had lost control.

"*What's happening?*" I asked.

"You are now the voice in *my* head," he said.

CHAPTER
SIXTEEN

Well, wasn't that freaking fantabulous? I tried to take a step back, but the command from my brain didn't reach my legs. In fact, the idea didn't even seem to register in my brain or anywhere else in my body.

"What the hell, Chaos? You said we had more time than this."

"Obviously, I was wrong." He made my voice say the words, and it was the freakiest thing I'd ever heard. Kinda like when you hear yourself on a recording, only way worse.

"Wrong about what?" Ember asked, but she didn't wait for an answer. She stepped into the room and headed straight for the niche in the far right corner where sparkles clung to a shape like glitter on a drag queen.

"Tell her." I tried again to control something on my body, but it was pointless. I couldn't even make my pinkie finger twitch.

"There's no skull here." We walked into the room and stood behind her while she stooped to examine a wooden box hidden by shadows.

"How do you know?" She waved her hand over the top of the box, thankfully not touching it. "It's sealed with magic. Maybe there's a cloaking spell on it too. Do your thing, and let's see."

Chaos inhaled deeply and exhaled slowly like he was fighting to hold in a growl. "We're wasting time here. We should move on to the next point of the star."

Ember looked over her shoulder at us. "What's gotten into you? Just do the spell so we can see. Skull or not, I want to know what's inside."

I started to recite the spell in my head, but Chaos cut me off and said it aloud himself. Nothing happened.

Ember narrowed her eyes. "Cast it for real."

"I can't use my magic unless I have control of my body. Give it back."

"I can't."

"Why not?" Ember asked.

"Why not?" I echoed her question. *"I was able to give you control for short times."*

"And that is what sped up the possession process. If I release control, we will bond even faster."

Ember blinked and tilted her head. "Is that what Chaos is saying?"

"Tell her."

He didn't.

Now it was my turn to growl. *"She needs to know."*

She stood, a look of worry creasing her brow. "Ash?"

Chaos tightened our right hand into a fist. "This body doesn't belong to Ash anymore."

"The hell it doesn't." She drew her sword, and flames erupted on the blade. "Bring her back now, or I'll..."

He crossed his...my...our arms. "Or you'll what? Stab your sister? Behead her?" He stepped toward her, and her hands trembled, the fire on the blade rolling back into her.

"Tell her I'm still here. You're scaring the bejeezus out of her."

He gripped the hilt of her sword and drew it from her grasp. She let him have it. Tears streamed down her cheeks, and she backed into the wall. "Ash," she whispered.

"Dammit, Chaos, if you don't tell her now, I'll..."

He chuckled. "You'll what?"

Friktity frak, he had a point. The demon was in complete control. Ember couldn't vanquish him without killing me. I couldn't control my body, so I was about as useful as mammaries on a man. Things just went from bad to the absolute worst they could be.

"Please tell her. I can't stand to see her cry."

He huffed, and the feeling in his bo...in *my* body—it was still mine, dammit, and I would regain control—went from *bwahahaha I'm finally free* to *wait, what am I doing?* "Ash is still alive for now."

Ember snapped her head toward him. "What do you mean, for now?"

"I have control of her body, but her consciousness is fully functional. Soon, though, my power will build, and her human form won't be able to hold me. She will die if we don't find my skull soon." He offered her the sword.

She yanked it from his grasp and held it at her side. "How soon?"

"A few hours. Maybe less, which is why we need to move on. My skull isn't here. I would sense it."

"It could be concealed." She gestured to the box. "Isabel was a strong witch. You said so yourself."

"You'll have to convince her if you're sure it's not here. She'll want to hack it open and release whatever's inside."

"Ash says you want to force it open." He kneeled by the box.

"She knows me well."

"Do you see this mark?" He pointed to a design carved into the wood. A series of crisscrossing lines and circles formed an intricate pattern about two inches wide.

"What about it?" She set her jaw, stubbornness obvious in her features.

"That is an adaptation of ancient Sanskrit combined with demonic sigils. It's a warning to her descendants that this one is a trap meant to kill any who attempt to free us."

Ember's eyes narrowed. "What would happen if I opened it?"

"Tell her that her face would melt off like the Nazis in Indiana Jones."

"Ash says your face would melt like something called a Jones Nazi." He rose and faced her.

Her eyes turned from narrowed in mild skepticism to slits of suspicion. "Is that what she says?" She crossed her arms. "Or are you just saying that? How do I know your skull isn't in there and you're saying it isn't so you'll get to take over Ash completely?"

"I want your sister to survive as much as you do." He raised a hand. "You have my word."

She blew out a hard breath. "The word of a demon doesn't mean much."

A spark of anger burned in our belly, the feeling both his and my own. *"She doesn't know you like I do."*

"You don't know me like you think you do."

Ember scoffed. "Then enlighten me, Mr. Prince of Hell. What's stopping you from trying to kill us both?"

He made my nostrils flare. "I was talking to Ash, but I will answer you. She and I share a bond. As long as it is intact, I will do whatever it takes to keep her safe...including taking out anyone who stands in my way."

"Jeez Louise. Don't threaten her, man. Ember loves to fight."

She tightened her grip on her sword, and flames licked down the blade. "And I suppose I'm in your way."

He closed our eyes, frustration, irritation, annoyance, and every other similar emotion flooding our system. "We are on the same side."

"No, we're not." She extinguished her sword and swung it at the box. Chaos caught her arm, keeping her from smashing it open, but the edge of the blade nicked the wood.

The magic surrounding the box pulsed orange before releasing a blast that knocked us on our butts. Chaos's demonic energy must've shielded us because he jumped to our feet and shook off the electrifying sensation crawling across our skin like it was nothing.

Ember didn't fare so well. She lay on her side, her eyes closed, her sword sticking into the dirt wall like a toothpick in a meatball.

Chaos grunted, the sound extremely strange coming from my body. "My skull isn't here. We need to get to the next point." He pulled the sword from the wall and scooped up my sister, carrying her as if she weighed no more than a ragdoll.

"Whoa. I'm not this strong."

"I am." He marched back through the corridor, following our path out of the mall and to the van. He put her in the back seat, and she groaned.

"What happened?" She rubbed her temples.

"You foolishly disobeyed me and tried to open the box. It fought back." He climbed into the driver's seat and started the engine.

"Whoa. You've been locked up since before electric lights. You can't drive a car."

"Your sister in is no condition to be behind the wheel. Your body has muscle memory. We'll be fine." He slammed on the gas pedal and peeled out of the parking lot. "Enter the coordinates for the next location."

Ember sat up and handed him her phone. "My head feels like it's going to split in two."

"If I had allowed you to hit it with your full strength, it probably would have."

Everyone was quiet on the half-hour drive to the next location, which gave me time to ponder why we even went to that mall in the first place. The reason was obvious. I didn't inherit the power from my dad like we hoped.

"Tell her I'm sorry."

"What are you sorry for?"

"Nothing." Ember scoffed. "I don't trust you."

Chaos flicked his gaze to the rearview mirror. "My question wasn't directed at you."

She leaned forward, resting her hands on the console. "Is Ash talking? What's she saying?"

"It didn't work. I took us to the wrong location. I don't have Dad's power."

He relayed the message and added, "But you did know exactly where to look once we got there."

Ember's head bobbed in the mirror. "He's right, Ash. Dad couldn't locate things miles away, either. If it was in the vicinity, he could find anything, and that's exactly what happened with you. Twice. I shouldn't have pushed you to do something he couldn't do."

"Listen to your sister," Chaos said. "She is correct."

"And anyway..." Ember leaned back in the seat. "These locations are protected with wards. We tried scrying for them and came up with nothing. Even if the power did work at a distance, you probably wouldn't have picked up on it."

"I suppose."

"She's reluctant to accept the reasoning." He made a sharp right, and the tires squealed.

"Careful."

Ember buckled her seatbelt. "She's always had self-esteem issues."

"They're unwarranted. Your sister is more powerful than she thinks."

"Everyone knows that but her." Ember's face pinched. "We have to save her."

"That's the plan." He hung a left, taking the corner more slowly this time.

"Fair warning," my sister said. "If we don't save her, and you take over, I'll vanquish your ass right back to that dark prison. Then I'll find your skull and pulverize it."

Chaos chuckled. "I would expect nothing less."

SEVENTEEN

"Now *this* looks like a place for a witch to hide a demon skull." Ember began strapping on her weapons before Chaos stopped the van.

The next point on the map had directed us to a massive field. A few gnarled trees jutted up from the knee-high grass here and there, their knobs and bumps and crooked branches giving the area a spooky feel, driving Ember's point home. This *did* look like a good place to hide a skull.

It felt like it too. A low vibration, almost imperceptible, hummed in the air, and as Chaos killed the engine and slid out of the van, the hairs on my arms stood on end.

Not that there was much I could do about it. With a demon in control of my body and my vim, I couldn't cast a spell to save my life. Kind of ironic because that was exactly what I needed to do. How the hell was I supposed to exorcise him if I was nothing more than a fading voice?

Worry about one thing at a time, Ash. First, we had to get the skull, and I was certain it was here. What I wasn't sure about was whether *I* knew it or Chaos did. I could feel his emotions, sense his power building as if we were the same person. He was essentially absorbing me into his consciousness, and the scary thing was...I felt at peace with it.

"*Why do I feel like ceasing to exist wouldn't be such a bad thing?*" I asked.

"That would be a *very* bad thing." He stomped through the grass toward an overgrown mass of vines and weeds. "You have to fight this. Don't give up."

Ember jogged to catch up, my potion satchel bouncing on her hip with each step. "Do you have anything in here for headaches?"

"*Tell her there's some pain powder in the blue pouch.*"

"Blue pouch," he said and continued his march toward the mess of brush.

Rage simmered in Chaos's chest, a barely contained inferno waiting to explode and take down everything in its path. Riding along with him in charge, I felt powerful...almost euphoric, which was weird because he wanted to tear Isabel and anyone else who knew about the skulls into a million tiny pieces and feed them to her descendants.

And if she wasn't turning to dust in a grave somewhere, he could do it. I had no doubt about that. Honestly, he'd be justified. I knew I was supposed to be about love and light...being a light witch and all... but the poor guy had been imprisoned for hundreds of years, all because a witch didn't want to pay when it came time to collect.

"It's here." He stopped a few yards away from the overgrowth, and holy Hecate, there was a building beneath all those vines. He started forward.

"Wait! Stop!" Ember ran towards us, fumbling with a potion bottle. "We need to see what spells are protecting it before you barge in."

Well, look at that. Leap-first-look-later Ember actually thought before she acted. *"She's right."*

"I can withstand any spell she could concoct." He kept marching.

"Whoa. First of all, my body can't. It's not just you running into the fray. And second, you obviously can't withstand anything, or we wouldn't be in this situation."

Something hard hit the front of our shin, sweeping our legs backward out from under us. We faceplanted in the grass, and I got a good look at what had hit us. Ember's boot.

"You're not running in there and putting my sister in any more danger than you already have." She dropped the bag on the ground, cocking her head as if challenging him. "Let me do this first. Tell him, Ash."

Chaos growled and stood. It sounded way less menacing than when he used his real voice, but Ember bristled.

She fisted her hands. "Do not make me knock my sister out."

"Get out of my way," Chaos roared and shoved Ember aside.

Uh-oh. My body would not appreciate what was about to happen next. Ember screamed like a Viking warrior and ran towards us. She bent at the last second, shoving her shoulder into our abdomen and dragging us to the ground. The air left our lungs in a whoosh, and if I were the one in charge, we'd have stayed down.

Chaos did not. He called on his demonic strength and literally threw Ember off us. She landed five feet away with a grunt, but she shot to her feet and came back for more. This had to stop.

"Chaos, cut it out."

"I'm sorry, Ash." My sister swung, clipping us in the chin. Pain exploded across one side of our face, but Chaos laughed in spite of it. Or maybe because of it. I wasn't sure.

The rage he'd kept at a gentle simmer began to boil. Our fists tightened, the muscles in our arms coiling. *"Don't hurt my sister."*

His punch landed dead center in her stomach. She doubled over with a groan.

"Stop it, Chaos. I mean it."

Her head snapped up, and she lunged. He swung our arm, flinging her away. *"Enough!"* I shouted in our head, but his demonic nature was in full swing. I had to take back control before he killed her.

"You're wasting time." I focused on the fire in the core of my being. It was still there. *I* was still there. I let it burn as hot as I dared and imagined it filling my body, flowing down my arms and legs, and I used that fire, my inborn gift, to seize control.

My muscles burned with the strength of my ancestors as I ripped my body away from Chaos and threw up my hands. "Stop fighting. Both of you."

My breath came out in a rush, and a maniacal giggle followed. I'd done it. I'd taken my body back.

"Ash?" Ember took a tentative step toward me. "Is it you?"

I parked my hands on my hips. "Yes, it's me, and I'm pissed at you both. You've wasted ten minutes fighting when I only have hours left. What were you thinking?"

Neither of them answered me, but I didn't have time to listen to their excuses, anyway. I turned toward the building in the brush. "Confess, expose my magic sleuth. I call on you to reveal your truth."

My head spun, but I shook it off and waited for the

golden dust to reveal what we were up against. It billowed like a cloud before swirling upward and descending over the structure like a dome.

"A cloaking spell? That's all?" Ember drew her sword and took a few cautious steps toward it.

I held out a hand to stop her and focused on the energy. One deep breath. Two. Then three. The low vibration I'd felt before hadn't grown any stronger. "Do you sense anything, Chaos?"

He was silent for a beat. Then he wheezed. *"You should not have taken back control. I can't hold back."*

"Oh, yes you can. Do you sense any demons close by?"

"The veil is thicker here. I don't sense anything but my skull."

"We're good." I nodded at Ember, and she slashed her sword through the spell, unraveling the camouflage. The decrepit building dissolved away, taking the overgrowth with it.

"Great. More grass." She sheathed her sword. "What now, Prince Harming?"

"He's in a timeout." My stomach rolled, and my peripheral vision grew hazy. His power was growing. I could tell he was holding back, but I had half an hour at most. "There has to be something here."

I swept my gaze across the grass and crept toward the space where the illusion of the house used to be.

"That was a powerful cloaking spell if it could change with time and the environment."

"We've already established Isabel was a beast." Ember searched the ground with me. "What are we thinking? Did she cast a circle or hide it underground?"

"Where's the bag? I'll check."

"Oh, crap. It's over there." She pointed behind us.

"I'll get it." I jogged to the bag, and by the time I got back to my sister, my muscles trembled. My hands shook as I uncapped the bottle of perimeter dust, and as I blew it toward the space, a hacking cough racked my lungs. Oh, lordy. I should not have done that. Every ounce of energy, every iota of magic dried up like a gully in a drought.

Ceasing to exist didn't feel peaceful anymore. It felt like getting hit by a train.

"What's wrong?" Ember clutched my shoulders and then pulled me to her chest. "Tell me what to do."

"Magic. Drained. My vim," I said between coughs. "Chaos."

"Is he coming back?" Alarm filled her eyes, and I nodded. "Okay. Okay, let's get the skull. Let's...shit. It's a circle."

"Holding in or keeping out?" My knees buckled for half a second before a surge of strength returned to my body. We stood, taking a step back, out of Ember's grasp, and straightening.

"I told you not to attempt regaining control," Chaos said with my mouth.

Fan-fluffing-tastic. The demon was back in charge.

"You were about to kill my sister."

"I wouldn't have killed her. Harmed her a little, perhaps. I was trying to subdue her."

"Yeah, well. You almost walked into a trap. You're welcome."

He sucked in an irritated breath like he was about to argue. "Thank you."

"Looks like we've got two choices." Ember drew her sword and eyed the perimeter. "Break the circle and risk turning loose whatever she has trapped in there, or step inside and take the chance of being stuck."

"Let's look at the pros and cons of each before we decide." I started to list them, but Chaos had another idea.

"Stay there," he said to Ember, and he stepped inside.

"What the eff, man? We're supposed to be working together." Ember fumed, but he ignored her, instead, locking his gaze on an area of disturbed ground.

"This is it. I can feel it." He kneeled.

I could feel it too. The pull in our belly like before, but also more. The vibration intensified, scattering my thoughts and sending my...our...emotions on a tilt-a-whirl. I needed to stop him. To insist he let Ember check the space for magic, but the desire, the need, was too strong. He...we...could finally be whole.

He felt the ground, swiping the dead weeds away to find a hatch. Anticipation built. I needed to say something, anything to caution him, but my scattered thoughts ping ponged off each other, making it impossible to think about anything but getting that skull.

"I'm coming in." Ember stepped toward the circle.

"Stay out!" Chaos boomed, stopping her short. "You will need to break this circle from the outside. The magic has trapped me in."

I wanted to argue that *we* were trapped, not just him, but he reached for the latch, gave it a twist, and opened the hatch. There, in the bottom of a rotting wood container, lay his skull.

This was too easy. I might not have been able to think straight, but the sinking sense of dread in my gut was unmistakable.

He reached inside. Something popped. A swarm of zombie fae shot out, slamming into our face and knocking us back.

"Son of a bitch!" Look at that. I'd found my words.

Chaos jumped to our feet and lunged for the skull, but the fae hadn't eaten in centuries. Did I ever mention how much they loved witch blood? And much like all the other creatures from across the veil, they didn't die unless they were beheaded, stabbed in the heart, or set on fire, so these suckers were ravenous.

They dive-bombed us, their tiny razor teeth slicing into our skin, taking little chunks of flesh before they retreated.

A few tried to escape, but the circle held them inside. They bounced off the wall and came back for us, more pissed off than ever. Chaos waved our arms, knocking them to the ground, but the starving little creatures would not be deterred. They wanted witch for dinner, and that was what they would have, goddess damn it.

"Ash! I'm coming in." Ember ran toward the circle. She slammed into the invisible wall, and dark magic pulsed, sending her careening into the ground three feet away. She landed with a thud, probably getting the wind knocked out of her.

Chaos kept swinging our arms, knocking the fae around, but they continued their assault. Our skin stung, and blood flowed in ribbons down our bare arms.

Ember tried again to cross the threshold, and again it knocked her back. Springing the trap kept anyone from getting in or out. Lovely.

Chaos roared, the sound way more guttural than I should have been capable of making. Our abdomen heated, burning hotter than my fire magic could go. He fisted our hands, crossing our arms in front of our chest. The heat felt like it would burn me alive.

Was this him taking over? Was he about to burn through my form and become a whole demon again? Goddess, I hoped not. Spontaneous combustion sounded like a painful way to go.

He roared again, throwing his arms out to the sides.

They erupted in flames.

He swung, moving faster than any witch was capable, turning into a tornado of fire inside the circle. Fae screeched, each one he hit tumbling to the ground, consumed by flames.

Exhilaration flowed through our veins, and I was pretty sure it was mine. My arms were *on fire*. Ember couldn't even do that. She could make fireballs and set objects ablaze like her sword, but this... Sure, it was the demon doing it, but holy Hecate, it was fun.

When the last fae hit the ground, its body shriveling and turning to dust, Chaos extinguished our arms and heaved in a breath. "Your body can't take much more."

"*No kidding.*" Fatigue replaced all the excitement. He heaved another ragged breath.

"I'm trying, Ash. I'm trying, but I'm failing." He scooped his skull from the hatch and tucked it under his arm.

"You're doing great. Look, you've got your skull. Let's put you back together."

He huffed. "Ember, you can break the circle now."

"Can I? It seemed pretty adamant to keep me out." She rummaged through my satchel for a dissolving spell.

"While she does that, let's exorcise you."

"We can't do it here. You must cast me out in the same place I possessed you if you want to survive the exorcism."

"Well, shit."

"Well said."

The drive home would be forty-five minutes at best. *"How much time do we have?"*

He hesitated to answer. "Not enough."

EIGHTEEN

"What's not enough?" Ember cast the dissolving spell and tore through the circle.

Chaos stumbled, and she clutched our arm, sending sharp pain shooting all the way past our shoulder, up the side of our neck, and into our head. He groaned. "Not enough. Time," he said through clenched teeth. "Get back...to house." Our knees buckled.

Ember clutched our shoulders, holding us upright. "Whoa, whoa, whoa. You are not burning through my sister right here in the field. You've got your skull. Do your thing."

"Can't do it here." He curled our hand, our nails digging into our palm.

My sister's lips parted, and her head wobbled like

a bobblehead doll as she put the pieces together. "Right. Okay, you have to return to the place where you two were bound in order for you to separate completely. We need the spell book too, though it wouldn't surprise me if Ash had it memorized. Let's go."

"I can't." We dropped to our knees. Pain ripped through us. Not hot. Not cold. Searing.

"Oh, yes you can." She tried to drag us up, but the pain overwhelmed us.

I could not go out this way. We'd come too far. We had the friggin' skull for Hecate's sake. If only Ember had teleportation powers, we could...wait.

"Can't demons portal through space?" My voice sounded strained even though my failing body didn't utter the words.

"Not in this condition." We dug our fingers into the dirt as another wave of pain crashed through us.

Ember paced in front of us. "C'mon, Ash. You're a problem solver. How do we fix this?" She dropped to her knees in front of us, pleading with her gaze. "How, Ash? Please?"

"Okay. Umm..." My thoughts swirled, scattering like billiard balls every time I tried to grab hold of one. If only I could freeze them in place for half a second so I could pluck a useful one from the fray. Yes! That was it!

"Tell her to freeze us."

"Will that work?" he asked, his voice thin.

"It's the only idea I've got, so let her have it."

"She says freeze us." We collapsed onto our side and curled like a fetus. I could feel his effort. The strain. He really was trying not to split me open and crawl out of my belly like an alien.

"Right. Of course." Ember turned my satchel upside down and shook it. Bottles clattered to the ground, and she spread them out. "I'll never make fun of your label maker again." She uncorked the bottle, said the incantation, and tossed the dust onto us.

Normally, the binding spell stilled the mind along with the body. I assumed since I was three-quarters of the way to becoming a full-blown demon, Chaos's magic fought against the enchantment. I wasn't completely coherent, but the feel of dirt and grass across my backside as Ember dragged us to the van set my nerves on edge. Too many friggin' fae bites to count sent screams of agony to my brain. I'd need to bathe in antibiotic ointment when this was done.

If I survived.

Ember leaned us against the front tire and opened the van door. Hooking her arms beneath our pits, she hauled us into the backseat. Bottles clanked against bone as she dropped my satchel, filled with potions and Chaos's skull, on the floorboard, and if I could have winced, I would have. No doubt she'd dumped everything into the center pouch, not bothering to organize anything, but I would deal with that mess later. Hopefully.

"Please let this spell last." She peeled out of the field, flinging gravel in her wake, and floored it.

"How's it going?" I asked Chaos, but he didn't respond. Ember's spell had rendered him mute like it should have, which was a good thing. The fact I was coherent enough to see the streetlights pulsing through the windows as we whizzed past, not so much.

It should have been a forty-five-minute drive back to Salem. Ember made it in thirty and thank the goddess she did. Right when she stopped in the alley behind our building, my pinkie twitched.

"Just hold on a little longer, Chaos." I had no idea if my words could soothe the savage beast he—we— were about to become, but I had to hold on to myself too. Talking in my head was the only thing I could do, so I turned into a chatterbox. *"Once this is done, I'll take you out for a steak dinner. Your resurrected body will be starving, right? Do you like beef? We could do seafood if you prefer, but I figure there aren't any oceans across the veil. Or are there?"*

"Here we go." Ember slid open the door and scooped me into her arms like a baby. If I'd had the use of my words, I'd have asked her why the hell she dragged me across the field if she was strong enough to carry me like this.

She finagled her arm just right so she could punch in the unlock code on the back door. She shoved it open and stepped through, but she didn't take my lolling head into account. My temple slammed against the jamb, and man, I wished I could groan.

"Sorry." She turned sideways and slipped inside, slamming the door shut with her foot before carrying me through the library and into my sigil studio.

Ember laid me and the skull on the floor and disappeared into the library before returning with her arms loaded down with supplies. "I'm going to put you in a circle before I unfreeze you."

Smart move. Who knew what condition Chaos would be in when he was finally free?

"I have to grab the exorcism grimoire. Give me two seconds." She darted out of the room again.

"*One Witchissippi. Two Witchissippi. Huh. She's late.*" Three fingers on my left hand twitched. Sadly, I was not the one controlling them.

My hand curled into a fist. "*Chaos...*" Molten lava churned in my chest. "*Please hold on.*" Hellfire rolled through my veins.

"Got it!" Ember raced in and opened the book on the table before flipping through the pages. "Here we go." She tapped the book and grabbed a canister of salt.

Speaking in Latin, she poured a ring around me, and I prayed to Hecate she was pronouncing the words right. Heaviness built inside the circle as she lit a bundle of sage and wafted it into the four corners of the room. Her voice grew in intensity. The energy inside the circle was suffocating.

"Okay." She set down the book and her supplies. "That should keep the demon in, but allow a witch to pass through. Is this the exorcism spell?" She held the book toward me, but I couldn't respond. "I'm unfreezing you in three, two...one."

She drew her magic inward, and we gasped. *"Yes, that's the spell."*

Dammit. Chaos was still in control. *"Let me take over."*

He groaned, tensing every muscle in our body. "I can't. I can't stop it."

"Then I will." I focused on whatever energy I had left. My own magic mixed with his, making it nearly impossible to tell my fire from the demon's. Maybe I could use that to my advantage. Did it really matter where the power came from as long as I could claw my way to the top?

No. No, it didn't.

I latched onto the heat, letting it fuel my consciousness. The hellfire raged, trying to consume me, but I rode it like a wave, letting it raise me higher.

"What. Are you. Doing, Ash?" Chaos ground out.

Ember lips curved into a half-smile. "She's digging her way to the top."

"Don't fight it. Let go."

"If I let go…" he said through teeth clenched like a vise. "You'll die."

"You're forgetting I'm a Holland witch. Let go."

He stopped straining. Our breath came out in a rush, and our body sagged. He sucked in a deep breath. The inferno roared.

I took the next breath. And the one after that. I scrambled to my knees, and Ember shoved the book toward me. I recited the words to rip him from my body, my mouth moving so fast I could have been speaking in tongues.

My muscles seized. I couldn't breathe for one second, two, three, four. Finally I exhaled and drew in another breath. I said the spell again. Then a third time, putting more vim than I had ever dared into the incantation.

A boom so loud it shook the house sounded from somewhere…inside me, outside, I couldn't tell. The sigil on my arm burned down to my bones, and if I didn't know any better, I'd have said my entire body turned inside out before righting itself again.

I gasped, my lungs tightening like I'd inhaled fiberglass, and when I exhaled, billowing black smoke rolled out of my mouth and nostrils to swirl around the skull lying on the floor.

Ember grabbed my arm and yanked me out of the circle while a storm brewed inside. Flashes of electricity pulsed and crackled. The dark cloud thickened, spinning like a tornado and gathering above the skull.

My sister's nails dug into my arm as we both stood there staring, unable to move.

The skull levitated, the tornado drawing it upward into the storm. The cloud took the shape of a man as the skull ascended. It billowed around the bone, and lightning cracked, blinding me for half a second. My vision wavered. The cloud dissipated.

My mouth dropped open at the sight of the demon.

CHAPTER

NINETEEN

"Release me!" Chaos boomed.

I needed to close my mouth, but my muscles wouldn't obey the command from my brain. Not because the demon had control, but because holy Hecate he was huge.

He stood seven and a half feet tall, with broad shoulders and a barrel of a chest. His skin, the color of red brick, stretched taut over the most defined muscles I'd ever seen. And his horns!

Thick, textured horns extended upward before curling around the sides of his head like a ram. My gaze drifted down his body to his... *Oh, my.* I swallowed hard, finally regaining my motor skills.

"Holy shit," Ember said. "That's what has been inside you all this time?"

I smiled. Hecate knew why, but I smiled. "Isn't he magnificent?"

"More like the stuff of nightmares." She clutched her sword and took two steps backward.

I moved toward the circle. "Chaos?"

"Don't get too close. That perimeter won't hold him forever."

"He won't hurt me. Will you, Chaos?" I didn't know why, but the temptation to step inside the circle and run my hand over his chest had me toeing the salt line.

"We had a deal, Ash. Let me go." His eyes glowed green, and his lips peeled back over pointy teeth.

"We need to vanquish him." Ember paced the perimeter of the circle. "It's too dangerous. I can feel his power from here."

He roared and lunged at my sister. She jumped like a frightened cat, but thankfully the circle held him in. "We had a deal."

"Okay, both of you, take a breath." I held up my hands. "Nobody's vanquishing anyone. We did have a deal, and I will uphold my end of the bargain once I'm sure you'll hold up yours."

His nostrils flared. "Of course I will."

"Don't trust him, Ash." Ember continued pacing. "Demons are liars."

"I'm not lying."

"How do we know?" I crossed my arms.

He closed his eyes like he was trying to calm himself down before he spoke. "We've been through this. You released me from prison. I am in your debt."

"Uh-huh." Ember stopped in front of him. "How do we know you won't be like Isabel and kill us so we can't collect?"

If looks could kill, Ember would've been nothing more than a heap of flesh. Chaos grunted at her and then looked at me. "Your arm."

The sigil pulsed deep red. "Why is that still there?"

"We are still bonded."

I rubbed the design as if it were drawn on with marker and I could smear it. Needless to say, my effort was fruitless. "Take it off."

He waited a beat, two, three before he said, "As long as it's there, I belong to you. If you're so concerned about me going back on my word, I suggest you keep it intact until this is over."

I laughed. "You belong to me? As in..."

"I serve you." He said it matter-of-factly like it didn't bother him the slightest that he was mine.

For some reason, it didn't bother me either. I had my very own demon. Woo hoo! "I believe him."

Ember looked at me like I was the one with horns. "He's manipulating you. He's been in your head too long."

"I'm not," he growled.

"He's not." I tilted my head at Ember. "Trust me."

"But how do you know?"

"I just do."

She waved one hand flippantly. "Whatever. But he better find Cinder, or I'm sending him back across the veil where he belongs."

"Great. Now there's just one more issue." I put my hands on my hips. "You're not going anywhere looking like that. You said you're a prince, right? Is there a human form lurking anywhere in there?"

He glanced down at his body, curled his meaty hands into fists, and smoke billowed around him again. When it dissipated, he'd shrunk to only six-foot-five. Thick, black hair replaced his horns, and sun-kissed skin covered his muscled frame.

My gaze wandered down his naked form, taking in the perfection that was Chaos. Heat pooled in my lady bits, and my stomach fluttered. When my eyes met his, I forgot to breathe. Emerald green with the same primal intensity as my dreams... Holy mother of magic, he was hot.

And, at least for the time being, he was *mine*.

A smirk lifted one corner of his mouth, and he arched a brow. "Is this better?"

I licked my lips. "Much."

ALSO BY CARRIE PULKINEN

New Orleans Nocturnes Series

License to Bite

Shift Happens

Life's a Witch

Santa Got Run Over by a Vampire

Finders Reapers

Swipe Right to Bite

Batshift Crazy

Collection One: Books 1-3

Crescent City Wolf Pack Series

Werewolves Only

Beneath a Blue Moon

Bound by Blood

A Deal with Death

A Song to Remember

Shifting Fate

Collection One: Books 1-3

Collection Two: Books 4-6

Haunted Ever After Series

Love at First Haunt

Second Chance Spirit

Third Time's a Ghost

Love and Ghosts

Love and Omens

Love and Curses

Collection One: Books 1 - 3

Collection Two: Books 4 - 6

Fire Witches of Salem Series

Chaos and Ash

Commanding Chaos

Claiming Chaos

Stand Alone Books

Flipping the Bird

Sign Steal Deliver

Azrael

Lilith

The Rest of Forever

Soul Catchers

Bewitching the Vampire

ABOUT THE AUTHOR

Carrie Pulkinen is a paranormal romance author who has always been fascinated with things that go bump in the night. Of course, when you grow up next door to a cemetery, the dead (and the undead) are hard to ignore. Pair that with her passion for writing and her love of a good happily-ever-after, and becoming a paranormal romance author seems like the only logical career choice.

Before she decided to turn her love of the written word into a career, Carrie spent the first part of her professional life as a high school journalism and yearbook teacher. She loves good chocolate and bad puns, and in her free time, she likes to read, drink wine, and travel with her family.

Connect with Carrie online:
www.CarriePulkinen.com

www.ingramcontent.com/pod-product-compliance
Lightning Source LLC
Chambersburg PA
CBHW030746190726
48285CB00003B/714